ACCEPTING

Slick Rock 8

Becca Van

MENAGE EVERLASTING

Siren Publishing, Inc.
www.SirenPublishing.com

A SIREN PUBLISHING BOOK
IMPRINT: Ménage Everlasting

ACCEPTING EVA
Copyright © 2013 by Becca Van

ISBN: 978-1-62242-440-5

First Printing: February 2013

Cover design by Les Byerley
All art and logo copyright © 2013 by Siren Publishing, Inc.

Printed in the U.S.A.

PUBLISHER
Siren Publishing, Inc.
www.SirenPublishing.com

DEDICATION

This book is dedicated to my son. He was born with congenital hip dysplasia and had many operations from a baby and hopefully suffered through the last one earlier this year. He is now eighteen years old and is one of the most gentle, caring human beings I know. I am very proud of you, Chris. I couldn't have asked for a better son.

Love always, Mum.xxoo

ACCEPTING EVA

Slick Rock 8

BECCA VAN
Copyright © 2013

Chapter One

She spun around when hands gripped her hips from behind. Her grocery bags landed on the ground near her car and she cringed, stepping away until her back came up against the cool metal body.

"Don't touch me again." Evana Woodridge glared at the man angrily. Why did men think they could do whatever the hell they liked? He raised his arms and held his hands up, palms facing her in a nonthreatening manner. He looked down at her leg and then back to her eyes and took a couple of steps back.

"I saw you limping and thought you may need a steadying hand." His gaze left hers and he stared at her leg again before sneering. "Obviously I was wrong." He turned and walked away without a backward glance.

Evana slumped against the side of her car and sighed over her reaction. She had nearly bitten the poor guy's head off. He probably was harmless and wanted nothing more than to genuinely help her, but he was a stranger and had put his hands on her. She didn't need his pity or anyone else's. She was sick and tired of being treated differently.

Looking across the parking lot, she met the eyes of a little boy being towed along by his mother. The boy was paying no attention to where he was going, staring instead at Eva. She was used to it and tried to summon up a smile for him. He looked up at his mom and asked loudly, "Mommy, what's wrong with the lady's leg?"

The woman glanced at Eva and then looked away just as quickly. Eva heard her mutter something to the boy, probably telling him not to stare, and then she tugged him away faster.

Eva sighed. She didn't mind curious children so much, at least she didn't now that she wasn't a child herself. Some adults were a lot worse, though.

She looked down at the two metal bars running parallel to the length of her right leg. They were attached to a special boot she wore and held in place by a sturdy leather cuff. She grimaced at it. Normally she didn't have a problem standing up for herself when people were rude, but today she just felt tired. She didn't believe in self-pity, but for just a moment she reflected on the twenty-three years of putting up with other people's hang-ups about her disability. It weighed her down.

She looked down at the grocery bags. A ready-made salad was visible in the top of one. Her stomach growled. *You're just tired and hungry*. Driving for two days to get to Slick Rock had taken a lot out of her. That was why she was feeling so disheartened.

Unlocking her car, she tried to cheer herself up. She was going to her motel room, where she could relax and plan out her sightseeing. She'd take a river tour and maybe indulge in a spa day at the Gateway Canyons Resort. The thought of someone pampering her by giving her a massage as well as a full-body treatment made some of the tension in her body ease. It had been nearly two years since she'd taken a vacation and it was beginning to show. She couldn't remember the last time she hadn't carried around any sort of stress. She was a stockbroker and had just been retrenched due to the worldwide economic downturn, which gave her the time she needed to take a break. Although she had loved her job, the stress had started to wear on her mind and body, and even if she could get employment with another stockbroking firm, Evana wasn't sure she wanted to.

"Are you okay, miss?"

Evana straightened and turned to face the man who was walking toward her. He was built! His shoulders were so wide she wondered if he would have to walk through a door sideways, but his strong chest tapered down to a flat, ridged abdomen and slim hips. The muscles in his thighs flexed beneath the denim of his jeans, and for such a big man, he looked graceful as he moved.

The man stopped a few feet away from her and perused her. Not once did revulsion or pity cross his handsome face. In fact his scrutiny was downright flattering.

His shoulder-length blond hair framed his square, rugged face, bristly with stubble, making his piercing blue eyes seem brighter. His height—he had to stand at least six and a half feet tall—and the tattoos she glimpsed on his muscled biceps made him seem slightly dangerous but no less enticing. She tried to peek at the design of the tattoos, but his tight black T-shirt covered most of them.

Evana cleared her throat and remembered that he'd asked her a question. "I'm fine, thanks."

"Do you need help getting your shopping into your car?"

Evana glanced down at the two bags she had forgotten were at her feet. She bent down and picked them up. "I've got them." She finally turned away from the drool-worthy man and opened the back door, placed her groceries inside, and closed the door again. When she turned around to face him once more, his eyes were glued to her lower body. *Has he been checking out my ass? No, surely not.* Most men ran away from her once they saw the bars on her leg.

He took another step closer and smiled in a chagrined kind of way, as if realizing that she'd caught him looking. Lifting his arm, he offered her his hand. "I'm Quin Badon. I run one of the car shops in town. I don't believe we've met before."

She took his hand and barely managed to hold in a gasp when warm tingles pulsed between their skin and raced up her arm. Quickly snatching her hand away, she opened her mouth, snapped it closed again, took a deep breath, and tried again. "I'm Evana Woodridge and I've never been here before."

"Well, I'm pleased to meet you, Evana. If you ever need someone to look at your car or to show you the sights while you're here, give me a call." Quin put his hand in his back pocket and pulled out a card. He handed it to her, gave her a mock salute, then turned and walked away.

Evana watched him go. He looked as good going as he did coming. His ass flexed and his shoulders rippled as he strode away with a loose-limbed gait. She sighed when he turned a corner and was out of her sight. *Did he just offer to take me on a date? No, Evana, get that thought out of your head right now. He was only being friendly.* She got into the driver's seat and started her car. After one more longing look in the direction Quin had gone, she sighed, put her car into drive, and headed toward the motel.

Although Evana was tired and wanted nothing more than to shower, eat, and curl up in the motel bed, her muscles felt too tight. Warm water only did so much, and she knew she needed to walk to stretch out her constrained muscles before she settled in for the night. It was late afternoon, but she still had at least another hour of daylight left. So after putting her salad in the small fridge in her room, she pocketed her key and set out on foot.

The Slick Rock Motel was on the west side of town but still close enough that if she decided to walk into the town center, she could with ease, most of the time. She'd also seen there were rooms to rent at the Slick Rock Hotel, but the thought of renting a room over a noisy bar didn't appeal. Apparently the motel was fairly new, so at least it should be clean and hopefully quiet.

Her right calf was tight after spending two days behind the wheel of her car, and experience warned that if she didn't stretch her muscles, her night would be spent in debilitating pain from cramping. She was just thankful she didn't suffer cramps as regularly as she had when she was a child.

Pain hit hard and fast. Evana cried out as her right leg collapsed beneath her. Her hands connected with the pavement, and the skin of her palms scraped on the abrasive surface, skinning them and her knees when the material of her pants shredded as she landed on all fours. Evana panicked slightly when she looked around. There was no one about since she had taken a route away from the town center. She had been so lost in thought she hadn't taken any notice of where she was walking. The only building in sight looked like a warehouse or a small factory.

"Damn, damn, damn," she muttered and eased onto her ass. She pulled up the leg of her three-quarter-length pants and quickly undid both the cuff below her knee and her boot. She pulled off the boot, taking her sock with it. Digging her fingers into the knots only helped slightly. She wasn't strong enough to massage the cramp away.

Pain shot from her calf and shin into her foot. The arch of her foot twitched and then contracted, making her toes curl under. Tears formed in her eyes and rolled down her cheeks. She hated giving into them, but the pain was so intense she couldn't ward them off. There was no way she could even stand when she was swamped with such agony. She sobbed and dug her fingers in harder, but nothing she did alleviated the pain.

The pounding of boots hitting pavement was only a vague distraction as she gasped and writhed. Strong arms scooped her up from the ground, and she looked up to see Quin Badon's grim face. "Put your arm around my neck, honey. I won't hurt you."

Evana did and then cried out as another excruciating cramp hit. Her body bowed, trying to get away from the discomfort, but she knew it was a useless endeavor. Coolness washed over her when Quin carried her into his shop, and then she was being lowered into a chair. He had brought her to the office off the side of his workshop.

"What's going on?" a male voice asked from the doorway.

She looked up through blurry vision and saw two handsome men looking at her with concern. She arched in the chair when more pain swamped her.

"Gray, get the hand wash from the bathroom," Quin ordered. He picked up her right leg, placed her foot on his thigh, and began to massage her calf.

Evana whimpered as his strong fingers dug into her contracting muscles. Even though it caused her more pain, she knew that eventually the knot would release and give her blessed relief.

"Can I do anything to help?" the other man asked.

"Yeah, go and see if we have something we can heat up," Quin replied. "Wait." He reached over to his side, pulled open a drawer in the desk, and grabbed a wheat bag. "Get this as hot as you can without it burning her and bring it back."

Evana closed her eyes and tried to relax her tension-wrought body. It was nearly impossible with the cramping. Gray came back and handed Quin the bottle of hand wash. He stopped massaging, squirted some of the liquid into the palm of his hand, and then rubbed his hands together. Once he had coated his skin, he began to massage her tight muscles once more. The liquid helped his skin slide over hers as he dug into the massive knots, and he used his thigh to put pressure on her toes, bending them back toward her shin and stretching her sole.

How long Quin worked on her she had no idea, but when the pain finally eased and then her muscles released, she was really tired. She slumped back into the large office chair and covered her mouth, hiding a yawn.

"Are you okay, Evana?" Quin asked.

"Yes." She opened her eyes and gave him a wan smile. "Thank you so much. I don't know what I would have…"

"I'm just glad I could help." He looked over toward the office door, and the other man handed over a hot wheat bag. "I'm going to tape this to your leg. The heat should help keep the cramps away, then we'll see about cleaning up your grazes."

"Oh." Evana looked at her palms. Blood was seeping out of her torn skin. She hoped she hadn't spread it everywhere when she had been in pain.

"Pierson, Grayson, meet Evana Woodridge. These are my brothers," Quin said as he taped the hot pack to her leg.

"Hi," Evana replied politely but kept her eyes lowered. She felt like a complete idiot now that her pain was gone.

"Let me see your hands, Evana. I'll clean them up for you." Evana looked up and went still. The brother Quin had introduced as Pierson had gold-green eyes. The color was so unusual, she couldn't look away. She felt as if she were drowning.

When she managed to take in the rest of him, she found that he was as well built as his brother. His muscles rippled and bulged as he moved. His six-foot-two frame had to carry over two hundred pounds of solid muscle. She raised her eyes to his light-brown hair and saw his lips quirk. When she realized she was staring, heat suffused her cheeks. She shielded her eyes with her lashes and turned her hands over for him to clean. Pierson swabbed her skin with antiseptic pads. The sting of the alcohol was nothing compared to what she had just endured, so she didn't even flinch.

Quin reached over and took another two packets from the first-aid kit Pierson had placed on the desk. He ripped one open and then cleaned her grazed knees.

"There you go. How's the leg?"

"Much better. Thank you," she replied, reaching for the tape.

A large hand covered hers. "No, leave it on, honey. The heat will help. Would you like a cup of coffee?" Quin asked.

She didn't feel up to walking back yet. "Yes, please."

Quin held her right ankle and maneuvered until he could reach another chair. He pulled it closer and then eased her foot down onto the seat.

"How do you take your coffee, Evana?" Grayson asked from the doorway. She drew in a ragged breath. All three Badon brothers were tall and ruggedly handsome. Gray had rich brown hair and brown eyes. His jaw was strong and square. Glancing between them, Evana noticed they all had indentations in their chins. Gray was taller than Pierson but shorter than Quin and no less muscular.

She found herself a little intimidated at having the attention of three such handsome, brawny men. Evana wasn't used to any attention from males unless it was in a derogatory or pitying way.

"White, no sugar, thanks."

"Do you get cramps like that often?" Pierson asked as he leaned against the edge of the desk.

"Yes, but they aren't as bad now as when I was a kid. Shit! I left my boot on the pavement." She went to get up but again was stopped when a large, warm hand landed on her shoulder.

"It's on the other desk, honey. Do you want it on?" Quin took a step toward the other desk.

"No. Not right now."

Gray entered the office with a tray loaded with coffee mugs. After placing it on the desk near her, he handed her a blue mug.

"Thank you," she sighed and wrapped her grazed palms around it, ignoring the slight sting caused by the heat of the cup.

Gray leaned against the desk next to Pierson, and Quin snagged the back of another chair and brought it closer to her and sat straddling it. Evana took a sip of her coffee for something to do. The three pairs of male eyes scrutinizing her made her feel a little uncomfortable.

"Sorry you had to carry me in here," she said.

"Don't worry about that," Pierson said.

"You don't weigh a thing," Quin added.

That might be true for men as big and powerfully built as they were. When they didn't say anything more, she found herself talking to fill the silence. "Once, when I was a kid, two of my friends had to carry me home from school because the cramps were so bad I couldn't walk. They made a seat for me out of their hands and carried me all the way home."

You're talking too much. But seeing that she had the total attention of her audience, Evana relaxed a little. "My mom had to spend an hour massaging the knots out of my leg that day. You guys got off easy."

Pierson smiled. "You were lucky to have such good friends."

Evana felt the warmth of that memory fade away. She wasn't sure she could count Tim as a friend anymore. "Yeah," she said weakly.

Tim had changed since he was a kid. Before she left Sheridan, Tim had been pushing her for a relationship. She had liked Tim when they were kids, but he seemed to have changed over the last few years and not in a good way. Before she had left home, she feared seeing him at all. Ever since her mom and Jack had left home to travel to Australia to see some of Jack's distant relatives, Tim had become a little too aggressive in his pursuit of her and she had become decidedly uncomfortable. As far as she was concerned, their friendship was no more, and in fact she had begun to fear Tim. So she had packed, locked up the house, and here she was.

She looked at the three Badon brothers, who still watched her intently. She wasn't going to burden these near strangers with her fears about Tim, not when those fears were probably unfounded anyway. She still had no proof it was him sneaking into her room at night while she was sleeping. A shiver raced up her spine, but Quin nudged her arm gently, pulling her mind from such distasteful thoughts.

Quin seemed to be scrutinizing her closely. "Can I ask you a question, Evana?"

Though she felt like she'd talked too much already, she said, "Sure."

"What happened to your leg?"

Chapter Two

Quin was aware that Pierson and Gray were giving him dirty looks, but he didn't see any problem with his question. Ignoring his brothers, he studied the petite, good-looking woman sipping her coffee. He wanted to know everything about her. When he had met her earlier that afternoon, he hadn't wanted to be too forward and scare her off, but now that she was in his office, he wanted to ask her everything. He was attracted to her and knew by the way his brothers were looking at her that they were drawn to her, too.

She wasn't very tall, standing at around five foot four, but she had a nicely rounded body. Her hips were voluptuous and she had a great chest. Her long hair shimmered even under the fluorescent office light, and he could see gold strands amongst the red. Her skin was a creamy white with a healthy tint of pink on her cheeks. There was a light dusting of freckles across her small, straight nose, which made her look younger than he imagined she was. Her eyes were a light shade of green, but he could see a few gold flecks in her irises.

As beautiful as her eyes were, it was her mouth that kept drawing Quin's gaze. Her lips were full and had a natural red tint, and all Quin wanted was to see her smile.

Right now she looked hesitant. It dawned on Quin that his question had been a little blunt and that was why Pierson and Grayson were still scowling at him. He tried to rephrase the question a little more tactfully.

"Were you in a car accident, Evana?" Quin questioned.

"No," she replied and hesitated as she leaned forward and rubbed her calf. "It's not a very interesting story, though. I don't want to bore you."

Quin looked at his brothers and back to her. *Why does she think she's boring?*

Before he could say something that would probably be tactless, Pierson said gently, "Quin didn't ask because we want an exciting story, Evana. We want to make sure you're okay."

Evana's first response was to blush furiously. Quin wondered about that, too. "Well, to cut a long story short, I was born with congenital hip dysplasia." She gestured down her leg. "My lower leg is bowed more than normal. It's also about a centimeter shorter than the left, though that's better than the two and a half centimeters' difference when I was a kid. The brace and bars help correct that, and the boot gives it some support. Sometimes I wonder if it's helped, though. I've still had a lot of surgery."

"How many operations have you had?" Gray asked.

"Um." She paused and looked like she was searching her memory. "About ten. I spent nearly five months in plaster from just below my ribs to my ankles with my legs out wide like a frog's. My mom said the cast was called a hip spica. And the second lot of plaster was from the top of my thighs to my ankles with a stick between my thighs just above my knees to keep them apart. Apparently that was so my hip socket had a chance to grow a little more, but it wasn't enough. The surgeon eventually had to do more surgery to make me one.

"That was major surgery and I ended up in bed in traction for six weeks and in a wheelchair for a while. I couldn't go to school for a whole semester."

"Shit, that must have been rough for a kid," Quin said.

"No, the operations I could handle fine. Thanks to my orthopedic surgeon, I may be able to keep my own hip joint for the next twenty years or more, though nothing's ever certain. I wouldn't even be able to walk if it wasn't for my surgeon."

"Why not?" Quin asked.

"I didn't have a formed hip socket. My surgeon made me a hip socket and put my femur back into place."

Quin was still curious, but Eva looked down at her coffee mug and said, "I've talked so much about myself."

"Not at all, sugar," Gray said.

"But we still have so many questions," Pierson said in a teasing tone.

Quin stood, realizing that they probably had asked her more than enough. He didn't want her to feel overwhelmed by them, but he didn't want her to go just yet. "We've finished for the day. Why don't you let us drive you to wherever you're staying?"

"Oh, thanks, but it's not that far."

"Are you staying at the motel, sugar?" Grayson asked.

"Yes. I plan on being in Slick Rock about two weeks." Evana leaned over to pull the tape from her lower leg.

"Let me do that, honey. I don't want it to start hurting you again." Quin began to peel the tape off her smooth skin. "We can't let you walk back to the motel by yourself, Evana. It'll be dark before you make it back."

"Oh!" She turned toward the window behind her. "I hadn't realized how late it was. Could you please hand me my boot?"

Quin walked over to the other desk, picked up her leg brace, and then handed Evana the boot and brace. He watched as she pulled her sock on and then her boot with the metal bars connected just before the heel. She opened the Velcro, placed the cuff below her knee, and secured it into place.

"What is the brace designed to do?" Pierson queried.

"Um, well, as I said, my right lower leg is too bowed. So the caliper helps keep it straighter and support and strengthen my muscles, and the boot is supposed to help keep my right foot from turning in."

"It always amazes me what specialists can do," Gray stated as he collected the empty mugs and placed them on the tray.

Quin knew that there was a lot more to it than Evana had explained, but she had given them the basics. He wondered how such a little thing had endured so much pain, but even as he thought that, he thought about all the other kids suffering in hospitals from life-threatening illnesses. At least Evana's condition had been corrected as she grew. A lot of other kids didn't have that kind of chance.

"Are you hungry, Evana?" Quin inquired as he led the way out of the workshop.

"Yes. It feels like I haven't eaten for hours."

"Come to the diner and have dinner with us," he suggested and guided her outside. He watched her nibble on her lip as she decided what she wanted to do and then she looked up at him with a small smile.

"I'll have dinner with you all on one condition."

"What's that, sugar?" Gray asked after pulling down the large roller doors to the shop and locking them.

"You let me pay. I want to thank you all for looking after me and helping me when I was in pain."

Quin looked at his brothers and gave them a wink when Evana looked away. If she wanted to pay for their meal, then he would let her. He didn't think she would accept their offer to dine with them if they refused.

"Okay, but the next meal is on us," Quin replied.

"Thank you."

Quin noticed that she didn't question the idea of there being a next meal. That seemed like a promising sign.

He took Evana's elbow and guided her toward his truck, and then he gripped her waist and lifted her up into the front before closing the door and skirting around to the driver's seat. She was buckling her seat belt as he got in. Gray and Pierson got in the back.

"What are you going to do while you're here, Evana?" Pierson queried as Quin started the engine and backed out of the lot.

"Please call me Eva. Most everybody does."

"Eva," Grayson repeated. "That's a lovely name."

Out of the corner of his eye, Quin saw her duck her head at the compliment. "I want to take a river tour, and I also want to sample the day spa. Other than that I have no firm plans."

"We could show you some of the sights if you'd like," Gray suggested, and Quin held his breath while he awaited her reply.

"You've already done so much for me. I wouldn't want to be a nuisance."

"You could never be that, honey." Quin glanced her way before turning his eyes back to the road. "Besides, we haven't been in town long ourselves and we want to explore more of the attractions."

"When had you planned to do the river cruise, Eva?" Pierson turned toward her.

"Um, on the weekend." She twisted in her seat to look at Pierson. "I wanted to have the experience when there were more people about. There is nothing worse than going somewhere touristy and being one of only a few people exploring. I love watching other people's reactions, too."

"We've been meaning to take that river cruise," Quin said as he pulled the truck into a parking space near the diner. "If you would like, we would love to come with you."

Quin switched off the ignition and turned to face her. She was raking her top teeth over her lower lip, and the urge to take her face between his hands and soothe her sensitive flesh with his tongue was nearly overwhelming. She looked adorable in her uncertainty, and he hoped she would take him up on his offer. He had never been drawn to a woman the way he was to Eva. It didn't matter to him that she wore a leg brace or had a slight limp. She was the sexiest woman he had ever seen.

She seemed like such a sweet, caring person, and although she looked uncertain and a little shy at times, he thought maybe deep down inside she could be feisty and passionate. The way she had insisted on paying for dinner for them helping her in her time of need showed him she wasn't selfish and she would probably be one of the first people to show up if called on in a crisis.

"Um, are you sure you want to do that with me?"

"Why wouldn't we want to, sugar?" Gray asked from the backseat.

"Well, most people don't want to be seen near me, let alone go out with me."

Quin bit back a curse. Eva looked so unsure and vulnerable. He wanted to rage at the people who had battered her self-confidence, but there was nothing he could do about her past.

But maybe he and his brothers could bolster her ego a little by spending as much time as they could with her over the next two weeks.

"We aren't most people, honey. We would love to escort you around and show you the sights. Why don't you think about it over dinner? Come on, let's go inside. I'll bet you're hungry."

Quin got out of the truck and waited for Eva on the pavement. Gray lifted her down, and Quin took her hand to lead her inside. He spotted a few of his friends and waved but didn't want to get into a conversation with them. He wanted some privacy while he got to know Evana Woodridge.

After seating her in the booth, he slid in on one side while Gray moved in from the other. She smiled at them all and picked up the plastic menu.

"All right, boys, what will you have?" The cheeky, shy smile on her face seemed to light her up from the inside. Evana practically glowed with life and vitality, which made her eyes sparkle. He could nearly imagine what she would look like in the throes of passion.

Quin shifted in his seat, pushing his lascivious thoughts aside, and concentrated on the woman next to him. A light, citrusy fragrance with a hint of vanilla assailed his nostrils. She smelled so nice, he wanted to lean down, place his nose against the skin of her neck, and inhale deeply.

"I'll just have the special, sugar," Gray ordered.

"What is the special?"

A waitress was just coming to their table for their order and heard Evana's question. "Today's special is meatloaf and gravy with vegetables."

"Make those two specials," Eva said.

After they'd given their orders and the waitress left, Quin sat back against the seat and studied Eva. From what he had seen so far, she was a complex woman, shy but sassy, with moments of bravado that couldn't hide her true vulnerability. Eva was the sweetest woman he had ever met.

"Where are you from, Eva?" Pierson questioned.

"Sheridan, Wyoming."

"That's quite a distance. You didn't drive all that way in one day, did you?" Quin questioned.

"No," she sighed. "I thought about it but knew it would be too much of a strain, so I did it in two days. But it didn't seem to make much difference."

"What do you mean, sugar?" Grayson picked up the glass of soda the waitress had placed on the table moments before.

"I have to be careful with the amount of time I spend inactive. I thought if I drove here in two days rather than one, I wouldn't suffer any cramping." Eva shrugged.

"What do you do for a living, darlin'?" Pierson leaned forward to see her around Gray.

"I'm a stockbroker. Or I was."

"Was?" Quin raised an eyebrow curiously.

"Yeah, I've just been retrenched."

"Shit, the economy is really struggling worldwide. So many people are suffering because the governments of their countries didn't make the right choices."

"Yes, it's pretty bad. I'm one of the lucky ones. I don't have a family to support."

"I'm sure you'll get a job with another stockbrokerage if that's what you want, Eva."

"That's another issue." Eva ran her finger over the rim of her glass. "I'm not sure I want to do that anymore. I didn't realize how stressed out I was until I was forced to take a sabbatical. Handling other people's money and trying to do the best for them in the market in this economic climate is just too much to deal with." She sighed. "But I'm not really sure what I want to do. I think I want something simpler and less stressful. Plus, I want to find a place of my own. My mom just remarried, and even though she and her new husband, Jack, are currently traveling, I want to give them time alone."

"I'm betting your mom loves having you around," Quin said with a smile.

"Yes, she does, but it's time I moved out on my own. I've depended on her long enough. She's worked hard her whole life, taking on two jobs to pay medical expenses and keeping a roof over our heads. It's more than time that I learned to stand on my own two feet."

"Are you going to live near your mother, Eva?"

"No!" Eva almost shouted her answer, and then her cheeks turned pink and she lowered her eyes.

Quin was taken aback at her reply. He had thought he'd almost seen fear in her eyes before she lowered them to the table. Opening his mouth, about to ask her what she was scared of, he closed it again when the waitress appeared with their meals. Once she left again, Eva looked at him and then his brothers.

"Sorry. I don't know what got into me."

Quin didn't believe her. The whole time she'd been talking to them, she seemed slightly evasive. He thought she was telling the truth about coming from Sheridan and looking for a chance to start over. What he doubted was the reason why.

What are you hiding, Eva?

He met her eyes for an instant, and then Eva looked away. Quin kept gazing at her, but it seemed like the subject was closed.

For now.

Chapter Three

Evana looked at the table again and cringed over her reaction to a simple question. The three Badon brothers must think she was a little crazy.

"Are you okay, sugar?" Gray asked.

Normally Eva would be perturbed over an endearment from a virtual stranger, but Gray had called the waitress "sugar," too, so she put it down to his friendly personality. In fact, all three of the men seemed to like using endearments when speaking to her. Quin kept calling her "honey" and Pierson had called her "darlin'" a couple of times. It made her feel warm inside and she secretly liked it even though they probably called all women such things.

"Yes. I'm fine."

The men began to eat, and she decided that if they could ignore her outburst, then so could she. She listened as the men spoke about their mechanic shop and how they had so much work booked in they didn't have time for any paperwork.

"What we need is someone to take over doing the books, schedule work, and order parts." Pierson sighed and picked up his glass.

"Yeah, you're right, but where the hell are we going to find someone with that sort of experience without having to pay a ransom for wages?" Quin pushed his empty plate away. "Even though we are running in the black and don't owe anything, we haven't been established long enough to hire an accountant with experience doing purchasing orders and reception duties. That is three different jobs, and we want one person to do that for minimum wage."

"I could do it," Eva blurted and then felt her cheeks heat.

She hadn't even known she was going to say that until she heard those four words coming from her mouth. Three pairs of eyes turned to her and pinned her with stares. Then Quin gave her a slow, wide smile. He opened his mouth, she was sure to accept her offer, but Pierson beat him.

"You're on vacation. You're supposed to be having free time. Why would you want to work?"

"I'm unemployed, not on vacation. Believe me, doing your office work would be like a walk in the park after what I've been dealing with." Eva knew deep down it was true. Now that she thought about it, she really wanted to help them out. They had helped her in her time of need, and she wanted to return the favor. She could still go sightseeing after hours and on the weekends, and if they accepted her offer she would have more time to stay in Slick Rock, away from Tim, and also to explore the area as much as she wanted while earning money.

Eva realized that she was thinking about staying in Slick Rock longer than two weeks. Sudden as the decision was, it felt right. She had a good feeling about this town and about these men in particular.

"You don't even know how much we're offering for the job," Gray said and leaned back in his seat.

Eva gave a nonchalant shrug. "I'm not worried about the amount. As long as I have a regular income and can find a place to stay, I'll be happy."

"That sounds like you want to stay here longer," Gray said.

Eva hesitated and then answered, "Maybe I do."

"Are you sure you want to do this, honey?" Quin reached for the hand she had placed on the table and took it in his.

"Yes." Eva felt warmth tingling up her arm and wanted to withdraw her hand, but she held still. She didn't want to let him know how much he and his brothers affected her just by touching her skin.

"We have a spare room," Gray piped up, drawing her gaze. She could have sworn she saw heat in his eyes, but it was gone within a heartbeat. Evana knew then that she must have imagined it. She looked back to Quin.

"Yeah, we do. That's a great idea." His thumb caressed the back of her hand, and goose bumps erupted on her flesh. A shiver of awareness coursed up her spine. Though she tried to contain her shuddering reaction, she wasn't quite sure she succeeded.

"Why don't Gray and I head on home and make sure everything is ready," Pierson said. "You can help Eva pack up and show her the way."

"Okay," Quin said.

"Thanks for dinner, sugar," Gray said, rising to his feet. Pierson was already standing beside their table. "We'll see you soon."

Eva watched the two men leave. All the Badon brothers looked like poetry in motion when they walked. She watched their asses until they were no longer in sight and then turned back to find Quin looking at her with an odd expression on his face.

"What did I just agree to?" She licked her lips and shifted in her seat.

"You are going to take our spare room," Quin stated, taking a firmer grip on her hand. "We can't offer you much of a wage, but we can offer you a place to stay. You are worth far more than minimum wage, honey. If you are going to be doing all our office work, the least we can do is have you living with us."

"That's not necessary. I can find my own place," Eva said.

"We know that, but we wouldn't feel right having you work for us and earning so little," Quin replied. "You would be doing us a huge favor, Eva. Please let us show you how much we appreciate what you are going to be doing for us by giving you a place to live."

Eva scraped her top teeth over her lower lip. She really liked Slick Rock and had felt the relaxed ambience of the rural town as soon as she had arrived. It would be so nice to not have to worry about looking for another job, and she had always wanted to live in a small town. Not that Sheridan was a city, but the small Colorado town just seemed to call to her. She would be safe here.

Only one worry made her hesitate. *They're being way too nice to me.* The only reason Eva could think of for their kindness was that they felt sorry for her. She wanted them to like her, not pity her.

But looking at Quin's face and seeing how eagerly he waited for her reply, she reconsidered. He looked at her as if her answer really mattered to him. As if *she* really mattered.

"On one condition." She looked up at Quin.

"Name it."

"You let me pitch in with all the chores."

"You're on." Quin slid from the booth and held out his hand toward her. Since Eva had already left money on the table for the bill and tip, she took his hand, stood, and followed him as he led her out of the diner.

They walked toward the motel. She felt comfortable in Quin's presence even though he was still holding her hand. Evana had only ever had one real boyfriend, and now that she thought back to her time with Shane, she realized he would never have been right for her. Shane had been a quiet, introverted person, and although she had liked him, she hadn't really loved him. She had been too young to realize that what she felt was forced on her part. Eva had been in love with the idea of being in love. Though she'd known the Badons a matter of hours, this felt completely different.

"How long have you been in Slick Rock?" she asked Quin.

"Eighteen months."

"Wow, and your business is already taking off. You must be very good mechanics." Eva turned and glanced up at Quin. "What did you do before coming here?"

"We served our country. Marines," he added.

That explains it, Eva thought. No wonder the three Badons had such confident, commanding personalities and buff bodies. They had spent most of their adult lives training and protecting their country.

"Why did you retire?"

"We served for over ten years, honey. We aren't getting any younger and we got sick of the traveling as well as the fighting. It was time for us to put down some roots and think about starting a family."

Does that mean they have girlfriends? Jealousy streaked through Eva, but she pushed it away. She had no right to be jealous of them. She'd only just met them.

"Um—I don't think I should live in your spare room."

"Why not?" Quin stopped walking and turned to look at her, a frown marring his face.

"You won't want me in the way if you entertain," she said diplomatically.

"We don't entertain, honey," he replied and then a grin spread over his face, wiping the frown away. "Oh, don't worry about us, Eva. None of us have any women in our lives. Besides, we like to share."

They had only just started walking again, but Eva stumbled over Quin's last statement. A muscular arm wrapped around her waist and pulled her against Quin's warm body until she was steady. When they began walking again, he didn't remove his arm. She inhaled his clean, masculine scent and then came back to what he had just said. When she looked up, she found Quin staring down at her intently.

"What?"

"I know you have only just arrived, but I figured I had better tell you from the start. There are a few unconventional marriages in town, and since we want the same kind of relationship, me and my brothers decided to move here."

Evana stopped in front of her motel door and stared at Quin. *Wait. Am I misunderstanding something? What did he mean when he said he and his brothers like to share?*

"What do you mean by 'unconventional'?"

"Ménage relationships are becoming more prevalent throughout the world or so I hear. Slick Rock has seven such unions living here. We are a very close-knit community and all look out for each other, especially the women. Females are the core to any relationship and since they are weaker than males, we all make sure they are protected.

"Gray, Pierson, and I decided we wanted such a relationship when were younger, and when we found out about the ménages in this town through some of our friends and realized we could actually live the way we wanted to, we decided this was the place for us."

"You want to share a woman, one woman between the three of you?" Eva's heart was racing with excitement, but she quickly tamped it down. She had only just met the Badons, but she liked them, a lot. Eva was drawn to them. The attraction was physical, yes, but there was more to it than that. It was way too early for her to even figure out why she felt the way she did.

She told herself to slow down. *Just because they have offered you a room in their house doesn't mean they want you, Eva. Look at you. Why would any man want a woman with deformities when he could have a healthy female?*

"That's the plan. We just haven't met the right woman *yet*."

Eva felt a slight pain in her chest. *See? You aren't even in the running, you stupid girl. You should know by now that men aren't interested in you.*

Eva pulled her room key from her pocket and turned away to open her door.

"Isn't that illegal?" she asked. "Having more than one husband, I mean."

Quin's voice was close behind and then the door closed with a slight click. "She can't marry all her men, if that's what you mean. Around here, the oldest brother marries their woman on paper. That doesn't mean she loves the others any less. As far as the lady and her men are concerned, she is married to all of her spouses in her heart, and vice versa. I have never seen happier people. The men dote on their wives, and the women love all their husbands equally."

"Don't the men get jealous of each other?" Eva went to lift her bag from the bed, where she had left it earlier, but Quin came up behind her and took it for her.

"Is this everything, honey?"

"Yes. Oh, wait. I have some groceries." Eva packed up the few things she'd bought at the market earlier in the day. "Okay, I'm done. I haven't unpacked anything else." She gazed into his eyes, wondering if he was going to answer her question.

He was so close that she could feel heat emanating from his body. She inhaled his scent again, this time picking up a trace of oil underlying his natural fragrance and light cologne. She liked it. It made her think of how masculine he was working with his hands, and the fresh aroma of pine and light tang of sweat drew her without overpowering his natural fragrance like some colognes could.

"The answer is no." Quin cupped her cheek. "I know a few of the men involved in such relationships and have talked to them a lot. They never get jealous of each other. In fact they are more than happy to know their women are safer. At least one of the men is always available to their wife to help her out with the kids if needed or just for a hug.

"Don't get me wrong, they have their ups and downs just like any marriage, but I have never seen women glow with love and happiness like the women of this town do. Men in polyamorous relationships get to spend time alone with their wife as well as all together. It seems to work out just fine."

Quin lowered his hand from her cheek and looked around the room. "Do you have everything, honey?"

"Yes." Eva sighed wistfully, wondering what it would be like to have the love and attention of more than one man. *Stop it, girl. You won't get the chance to have one man, let alone three.* The polyandrous marriages in town didn't shock her much, now that she'd had a moment to think about them. Although it was unusual, Eva didn't care how other people lived their lives. Her motto was as long as no one got hurt, live and let live.

Pushing her thoughts away, she wiped all expression from her face and headed toward the door after picking up her purse. "I need to go to reception and pay for the night and sign out."

"This is your car, isn't it?" He gestured toward the late-model sedan outside the room. "If you give me your keys, I'll stow your bag." Quin closed the door behind him.

Eva handed the keys to her car to Quin and headed for the reception office. Once done, she headed back out to her car. The revving of an engine drew her gaze and then a dark sedan peeled away from the curb with a squeal of tires. She'd only caught a glimpse of the driver, but he had looked a little like Tim.

She stood staring after the car until the taillights were no longer in view. *You're imagining things, Eva. That wasn't Tim's car. It was a rental. Tim would never drive a rental. He loves his truck way too much to drive anything else. There is no way he could have followed me. I didn't tell anyone besides my mom where I was going.*

He may have been a little obsessed, but there was no way he would have followed her. Tim had a cash transport business to run and he was a workaholic. There was no way he would have taken time off to follow her. *Would he?*

Chapter Four

Gray was nervous but excited about Eva coming to stay and work with them. She seemed to have such contrasting personalities and he wanted to get to know her better. One minute she was shy and uncertain, and the next she was sassy and vibrant. He and Pierson had raced through the house making sure everything was tidy. They weren't messy men, but every now and then they left things out just like anybody else. After making the bed up in the spare room, he checked the bathroom. There were a couple of towels lying on the vanity and another on the floor. After scooping them up, he raced to the laundry and then went back to the bathroom to put out fresh towels. He and Pierson shared the main bathroom, whereas Quin had one off the master bedroom he occupied.

"Everything set?" Pierson asked when Gray entered the kitchen.

"Yeah." He leaned against the counter, folding his arms to stop himself from fidgeting. Pierson, he noticed, looked a little anxious, too. He turned toward the coffeepot and checked it. With his back still to Grayson, Pierson said, "She's pretty, isn't she?"

Gray stood up a little straighter. Was it possible that his brother was thinking what he was? "You think so, too?"

Pierson turned. Gray thought that he saw relief in his brother's eyes. "She's beautiful," Pierson said. "You think she's the one?"

The one. The reason they were in Slick Rock. And she'd come right to their doorstep.

It seemed almost too good to be true. Gray felt cautious. What if they all fell for a woman who wasn't even sure if she'd stay in Slick Rock for good?

"We'd better go slow," he warned. "Eva's probably never even thought about being with more than one man before."

"Sure, sure." Always impatient, Pierson waved away Gray's caution. "But you think she could be the one?"

"How the hell should I know? It's way too soon to tell." Hearing his words come out sharper than he'd intended, Gray sighed and scrubbed a hand over his face. "Sorry."

"Don't worry about it." Pierson eyed him and then smiled to relieve some of the tension. "I'm feeling just as het up as you are."

"Any idea if Quin's on board?"

"No. But you know how he is," Pierson said. "If he's interested, he'll tell her we want to share a woman."

"We both know how he'll go after something he wants. He never was one to be diplomatic."

"Let's just hope he hasn't scared her off with his honesty." Pierson looked uncharacteristically dour. Glancing beyond Gray, he added, "That's them."

Headlights passed through the kitchen window as a car pulled into the drive. Gray looked out the window and started to feel excited again. "I think he'll be more careful about what he says to Eva. He wants her just as much as we do."

"You think so?" Pierson sounded hopeful once more.

"Only one way to find out."

Pierson placed his mug on the counter and headed for the back door. Gray decided he wanted to see Evana as she got out of the car. If she looked shell-shocked, then he knew Quin had broken the news about the ménage relationships in town.

Quin got out and was headed around the front of Eva's car to help her out, but before he could she made her way toward the house. Gray searched her face and saw she didn't look nervous, anxious, or in shock. What surprised him was that her face was expressionless. He had learned that Eva had a very expressive face but her eyes were the window to her emotions. When he looked at Quin, his brother gave him a slight nod and shrug of his shoulders.

Gray wanted to ask Quin what he had said to Eva but was going to have to wait for them to have some time away from her before he began questioning his brother. He smiled at Eva when she turned toward him. She was small. The top of her head only reached to just below his shoulders, and he wasn't even as tall as Quin. He hoped their size didn't intimidate her. Stopping a few steps away, he lifted his hand, lightly clasping hers when she mirrored his gesture.

"Come on into the house, sugar." Gray led Eva toward the back porch. "Quin will get your things. Would you like a drink?"

He watched as she looked around. Her eyes lit up when she saw the black granite countertops and the latest stainless-steel appliances and high-gloss white cabinets.

"Wow, you guys have the best kitchen."

"Do you like to cook, sugar?"

"Yes, I do. I didn't get much of a chance though. I was always working such long hours and Mom worked two jobs for a long while, but when she met Jack and he moved in, she didn't have to work anymore so she did all the cooking."

"Feel free to cook anytime you want, honey," Quin said with a grin as he entered the kitchen.

"Thanks."

"Come on and let me show you the rest of the house." Gray led her through the house, showing her where everything was. Once done, he led her back to the first bedroom near the start of the hallway, which was just off the huge living room. "This will be your room, Eva. I'm sorry you don't have a private bathroom and will have to share with myself and Pierson."

"You're kidding, right?" She gave him a wry smile. "This room is much larger than mine back home, and since my mom's house was small, I'm used to sharing a bathroom."

"Where do you want your bag, darlin'?" Pierson asked as he came into her room.

"Just put it on the bed, thanks. I'll unpack later."

"Coffee's ready," Quin's voice called loudly.

* * * *

Evana led the way back to the kitchen and sat down at the table where Quin indicated. She was aware of the three men watching her as she sipped her coffee. Looking up she saw three pairs of heated male eyes giving her body the once-over. Shifting in her seat, she nearly grimaced as her damp panties rubbed against her labia. Never had she dreamed that one man would have the ability to turn her on so much, let alone three.

And it wasn't just what they did to her sex drive. All three Badon brothers were really nice men and she was drawn to them. She was so hot for them it was a wonder she didn't have smoke coming out her ears. Her desire for them was so great that her body felt overheated, and she had the urge to jump their bones. Not that she would. Eva had never been forward when it came to the opposite sex. The only time she became a little feisty or snarky was when she got stared at.

The way the men were staring at her now, however, was totally new. "What?" She finally found her courage and voice.

"Don't you know how attractive you are, honey?" Quin asked and continued when she gave a slight shake of her head. "You have such beautiful red hair and green eyes, and your skin looks so soft and creamy."

Eva wasn't sure how to respond to that, but her body had no problems. Her breasts swelled and her nipples hardened. The ache in her pussy and clit intensified, her inner muscles clenched, and more of her juices leaked out. "Uh−I…thanks."

Gray cleared his throat, drawing her attention. "We want you to make yourself at home here, sugar. Just treat our house like you would your mom's."

"Okay. Thank you." She looked into her mug for something to do. "What time do you want me to start work tomorrow morning?"

"We start between six thirty and seven, depending how much work we have on for the day. You don't have to come in that early. Why don't you start at eight?" Pierson suggested.

"I can start early, too." Evana covered her mouth as a yawn slipped out. "I think it would be best if I start when you guys do for a while. That way I'll be able to set everything up and ask you questions if need be."

"You don't have to, Eva," Quin said. "We will still be in the shop whether you start early or not."

"I know, but I'm an early bird. I'd rather do something constructive than sit around here watching the clock."

"All right, we'll be ready to leave by a quarter after six. If you want a lift with us, be ready by then."

"Okay. I think I'll head on to bed." Eva wished she knew how to properly thank them for their kindness. "I'll see you in the morning. Good night."

Evana didn't look back as she left. Their voices carried down the hall to her room, though she couldn't hear the actual words spoken. All she wanted to do was crawl into bed and sleep, but first she needed a shower. She went into the bathroom and stood for a moment looking at the toothbrushes and razors that must belong to Gray and Pierson. It brought home the fact that she was staying in the house of men she just met. Even more disconcerting was her attraction to all three men, and brothers at that, because besides the one boyfriend she'd had in college, she'd never had another relationship with a man. Now that Quin had told her he and his brothers were looking for a woman to share, her imagination was in overdrive.

The thought of three sets of hands, as well as three mouths and cocks ready for her pleasure, was just too much for her to comprehend. Closing the bedroom door, she unpacked her clothes and then headed for the bathroom. After showering, she crawled into bed and closed her eyes. Her mind was racing a mile a minute and Eva knew it was going to be quite a while before she could fall asleep.

The fear that Tim had followed her wouldn't relent. Over the last few months his weird behavior had escalated, but what frustrated Eva the most was she never caught him in the act. A shiver of fear raced up her spine. He had been in her bedroom in the dead of night and left things for her, yet she never heard him. Had he watched her while she slept?

Another shudder wracked her body, but this one was revulsion rather than fear. She couldn't prove it was him leaving things for her, and even though she had wanted to tell her mom, she couldn't. How could she accuse her neighbor of such scary, revolting actions if she didn't have any proof?

* * * *

Pierson waited until he heard Evana's footsteps in the hall. He turned to Quin. "Okay, what did you tell her?"

Quin frowned. "Tell her about what?"

"Quit screwing around, Quin." Pierson felt like he'd waited long enough to find out what had happened on Quin and Eva's car ride. "Did you talk to her about Slick Rock?"

Instead of answering, Quin kept on frowning. "I'm not screwing around."

Gray, as usual, acted as the voice of reason. He held up a hand to Pierson. "Let Quin talk."

Pierson tried to rein in his impatience, folding his arms across his chest.

Gray turned to Quin. "What did you say?"

"I said that folks in this town like ménage relationships, and then I told her we moved here because we wanted that kind of marriage, too." Quin gave a rare smile. "She tried to back out of staying here."

"Why?" Pierson asked.

"I told her we wanted to share a woman, and she got nervous. She was scared she would be cramping our style by staying with us. I let her know none of us were involved with anyone and we hadn't found the right woman yet."

Yet was the operative word, as far as Pierson was concerned.

"How did she react?" Gray asked.

"At first she looked a little sad. She tried to hide it, but she has very expressive eyes." Quin's smile broadened. "But she wasn't shocked for long. I think she imagined the three of us with her."

"Shit." Gray shifted in his seat. "Don't even go there."

"Sorry." Quin grinned but didn't look apologetic at all.

"What else?" Pierson pinned Quin with his gaze.

"She asked if the men got jealous of each other, but I set her straight. She didn't say much after that. I think she was still processing the information."

"Why do you think she got sad?"

"I don't know. We are going to have to let her lead us in this. I don't want to scare her off."

Despite his cautious tone, Pierson wanted to leap up and run a victory lap around the block. All three of them had been drawn to Eva, and all three of them wanted to show her what life in Slick Rock could be like.

"We hear you, Quin, but what if she doesn't want to be with us? What if she doesn't make a move?"

"Back off, Gray. We're just as eager as you are, but we've known Evana only a few short hours. We need to go at her pace. From what she's said about her childhood, her self-confidence has taken a pounding. If we push too hard, too fast, she'll leave."

"I think we'd better pick up some liniment and massage oils. Eva obviously suffers debilitating cramps. I was really worried about her. She looked like she was in agony. I couldn't stand seeing her cry."

"Yeah, I hated it, too. Good idea, Pierson." Quin scrubbed a hand over his face.

Pierson was glad that Eva had agreed to live and work with them. Now that they had her in their lives, he and his brothers would be able to gently woo her. Knowing Quin was just as attracted to Eva as he and Grayson were pleased him to no end. He felt it in his heart all the way to his bones that Eva was the woman they had been waiting for.

Although his mind was racing, his body was tired. A yawn caught him, and he rose to his feet. "I'm going to bed. I didn't get much sleep last night."

Pierson closed the door to his room and listened intently, trying to hear if Eva had settled or was still moving around. When he couldn't hear anything he gathered up some clean boxers and headed to the bathroom. He was so tired he wanted to sleep for a week, but he knew that wasn't about to happen. They had so much work at the garage they could barely keep up, and they weren't the only mechanics in town. Sam Osborn ran the other mechanic shop and he had also served in the marines. He was a good friend. Sam and his brothers, Tyson and Damon, were involved in one of the town's ménages, and though Pierson was happy for them, he envied them, too. In fact he was feeling rather jealous of all the men involved in ménage relationships, because that's what he wanted more than anything else.

His thoughts turned to Evana. She was such an enigma, yet he felt like he had known her forever. Eva was so small compared to him and his brothers, and although he wanted to take her into his arms and kiss and hug her, he was almost frightened he would hurt her. She seemed so fragile compared to them. He was so eager to begin courting her but scared of making her run by being too fervent. Sighing, he made his way to the bathroom to shower.

As he stood under the warm spray he went back over what Quin had said. They were going to have to let Eva take the lead. Hopefully she wouldn't take too long to make a move, because he was too impatient to wait very long. And how the hell were they going to get a shy woman to make a move on three tall men?

Now there's a million-dollar question!

Chapter Five

"There she is." Pierson's teasing voice was the first thing to greet Eva as she entered the shop. "Wandering in late as usual."

He wiped oil off his hands with a rag, grinning at her as he rounded the front of the truck he was working on. "That coffee better be for me."

She held her coffee away from him as he playfully reached for it. "I am not late," she said. "It's exactly eight o'clock."

"Yeah, but some of us have been here since six thirty, lazy bones."

"Lazy bones!"

"Pierson…" Gray sighed as he walked into the garage from the offices. "Leave her alone. It's too early."

While she was distracted, Pierson grabbed the coffee out of her hand. "Hey!" Eva said.

He slurped it noisily. "Mmm."

"Don't be disgusting." Laughing, she slapped him on the arm. "There are three cups for you and your brothers in the car."

Pierson looked a little sheepish and gave her back her cup. "Why didn't you say something sooner? Don't stand between a man and his coffee, darlin'. Come on, I'll help carry them in."

He led the way out to her car. On her way out, Eva glanced over her shoulder toward Gray. She caught him watching her. Though he quickly returned his attention to the clipboard in his hands, she would have sworn his look was heated and appraising.

It wasn't the first time in the past two weeks that she'd caught one of the Badon brothers looking at her like that. Though they treated her with respect and courtesy, the way they watched her made her wonder.

You're imagining things. She watched Pierson open up her car door and retrieve the coffees. They were just considerate men. That was all.

When Pierson straightened, he handed her a cup. Even after she took it, his hand lingered on the paper cup until Eva raised her eyes to him. "You do know I was just teasing you, don't you, darlin'? We know how hard you work."

His sweetness kindled a warmth in her chest. "Thank you, Pierson. I know."

"Our office has never been as organized as it is now." He shut the door with his hip, and they began walking back to the garage. "You deserve to relax a little if you want to."

Eva didn't want to tell him so, but she actually missed them when she was in the house alone each morning. She knew she was beginning to feel too deeply for each of them, and it worried her that the longer she stayed with them the more she became emotionally attached.

"And you ought to get your sleep," Pierson added a little pointedly.

She didn't acknowledge that remark. She wasn't sure how Pierson knew she hadn't been sleeping well, but she was trying to avoid discussing it. Last night he'd sent her off to bed after dinner, even though it had been her turn to clean up the dishes. When she had argued he had just taken her gently by the shoulders, turned her in the direction of her bedroom, and given her a small shove, and all without saying a word.

Now, however, he relented and his sunny nature reasserted itself. "Thanks for the coffee, darlin'," he said with a wink and returned to his work.

Grayson gave her a smile when she offered him a cup. "Thanks, honey. Oh, before I forget, the bulb is out in the office closet. I'll change it later."

"Don't worry about it. Where's Quin?"

"He's out giving an assessment on a wrecked car. Should be back in a bit."

"Tell him there's coffee for him in the office if he wants it."

"If you made it, I know he will."

She went off to the office with a warm feeling in her chest. She really felt like she'd bonded with Gray and Pierson. Pierson was one of those men who would give her his last dime if she needed it and be happy about it, not caring that he didn't have anything left for himself. And Gray always seemed to be finding reasons to pop into the office and check on her. Smiling to herself as she turned on the computer, she wondered if he'd loosened the bulb in the closet just to have an excuse to come fix it and then hang around and talk to her. Well, he would have to come up with a different reason, she thought, because she was perfectly capable of changing a lightbulb.

Leaving the coffees on the desk, she dragged one of the chairs into the closet and climbed up. When she wobbled, she had to stabilize herself on one of the shelves. She was reaching for the blown lightbulb when a harsh voice said behind her, "What the hell do you think you're doing?"

Quin gripped her hips. Eva hadn't heard him come in and his voice startled her. She would have taken a tumble from the chair if he hadn't been holding her. But his tone of voice put her on the defensive.

"What does it look like I'm doing?" She frowned down at him, but he didn't let go of her hips. Even if he looked mad enough to spit, she couldn't help but think how good his big hands felt on her.

"Don't you get sassy with me, little girl. Get down right now!" His cold-as-steel voice sent shivers racing up and down her spine. Good shivers.

With slow deliberation she stepped down from the chair, his hands still on her hips. Back on the ground, she turned around to face him. He looked furious.

"What is your problem? I was only changing the bulb."

"You will never do anything like that again, Eva. You put yourself in danger. Next time, you ask one of us to do it for you."

Eva bristled. She had seen Quin do this before. One moment he was the most considerate, chivalrous man she'd ever met, and the next he was a ball of overprotective rage. And she didn't need it. "I'm quite capable of—"

"I don't give a fuck," he snarled.

Eva stared at him, shocked. Quin seemed to come back to himself. He released her and took a few steps back. "Sorry, I can be pretty aggressive."

"You think?"

His eyes narrowed again. "Watch that tone, honey, or you're going to find yourself facedown over my knee."

Astonishment stole her ability to reply for a moment. Her shock was followed almost at once by arousal. Heat flooded her at the thought of Quin throwing her over his knee. *What is wrong with you, girl?*

There was a wicked gleam in Quin's eye that made her wonder if he didn't find that thought alluring, too. Mostly, though, he looked mad. "What did you say?" she asked.

"You heard me, Eva. Let's get a few things straight. I don't want you doing anything dangerous. What if you had fallen off that chair and hit your head on the corner of the desk? If you fell while one of the compressors was on in the shop, we wouldn't have heard you cry out. You could have broken your neck and would have lain there on the floor, injured or dying, and we wouldn't have been able to help you."

Eva had to admit that he had a point, but she and her mom were so used to doing everything in the house, since there had never been a man around, that she hadn't thought to ask for help. "Then next time I'll ask for help." She wanted to stand up to him but felt shy. She lowered her eyes and continued, "And next time you won't swear at me when you lose your temper."

Quin cupped her cheek to raise her eyes to his. "I'm sorry I yelled at you, but you scared me when I saw you up there. That chair has wheels on it and it could have rolled out from under you."

Eva stared at him, his words rolling around in her head, until she had to ask. "You wouldn't really spank me, would you?"

Was she imagining the passionate look that came back into his eyes?

"You'd better believe it, honey." He dropped his hand and gave her a wink. "Let me take care of that blown bulb."

* * * *

Eva didn't get much done for the rest of the day. She spent way too much time staring through the office door into the garage for glimpses of the Badon brothers. Long after Quin had gone back to work, her body yearned to find out what it would be like to have his hands on her ass. If the phone hadn't rung occasionally, she probably would have sat in a sexual haze for hours.

By the end of the day, though, her smoldering arousal had cooled and reason began to prevail. *I'm way too attached to them.* Each man, in his own way, had captured her heart. Each day she fell a little more in love with them. *What the hell am I going to do when they don't need me anymore?* Even if they'd gotten used to having her around the office, that didn't mean that she was a part of their lives. Could she stand by and watch them fall in love with someone else while she remained their office manager and a perpetual spinster?

Eva shoved her depressing thoughts aside and shut the PC down. She looked around, making sure everything was away and the answering machine was on, then picked up her purse and headed out.

"Are you done, sugar?" Gray came toward her drying his clean hands on a towel.

"Yeah, I am going to stop at the supermarket to pick up something for dinner. Do you have any preferences?"

"No. Whatever you cook tastes good, Eva." He winked at her. "I'm going to have to watch my waistline with you around."

Eva eyed his stomach and chest and gave a snort. "Yeah, right. If you were any more buff and handsome, you'd have to beat women off with a stick. You probably do already."

Her cheeks heated when she realized what she'd said and she lowered her eyes to her feet. *God, Eva, think before you open your mouth.*

Pierson's feet came into view. Before she realized he was even in the room, he was so close she could feel his body heat. "Do you think I'm handsome, darlin'?"

Is he for real? Why would he ask me that? He and his brothers were so muscular and ruggedly handsome she got wet just by being near them.

She looked up at him and saw heat but also vulnerability in his eyes. It seemed he wasn't as confident as he made out. Drawing in a deep breath, she decided to be honest.

"Yes, you're handsome. All of you are."

He searched her eyes and then, without any warning, leaned down and placed his lips on hers. Pierson wasn't aggressive. He just brushed his soft lips back and forth over hers as if testing for a reaction.

Her body sure gave him one. Eva tried to conceal the shudder working its way up her spine as cream leaked from her pussy. Awareness washed over her in heated waves. Gasping in a breath on a sob, she held still, not knowing how to react or what to do.

A low, groaning rumble sounded from deep in his chest, and he wrapped his arm around her waist, drawing her against his hard, warm body. He walked her backward a couple of steps, and her shoulders came up against the timber doorjamb. Pierson slanted his mouth and deepened the kiss. His tongue swept over her lips and then thrust into her mouth. Eva sobbed as he slid his tongue along hers and then explored every inch of her mouth. She clung to his bulging biceps, the only anchor in a world gone mad with desire.

Never had she been kissed with such passion, such hunger. Her body ached, craving more of his touch. He tasted of coffee and mint, and she yearned to taste more of him. Eva wanted the kiss to go on and on. She couldn't prevent a whimper of protest from escaping when he slowed the kiss down and finally lifted his head.

"That was fucking hot." Quin's voice came from close by. Eva looked up with embarrassment at being caught kissing his brother. "Come here, Eva." His voice was deeper and huskier than normal, and although she hated to obey a command, she found herself moving on wobbly legs toward him when Pierson released her and stepped back.

"I want a kiss, too, honey. Will you let me?"

Shivering with need, she opened her mouth but couldn't seem to find any words. Staring into his hungry eyes, she nodded.

He moved fast for such a big man. One instant he was still several feet away and the next he had her in his arms. Quin wasn't tentative at all. Slamming his mouth over hers, pushing his tongue between her lips, he ravaged her. She was only vaguely aware that her feet had left the floor. Her hands gripped his solid, strong shoulders, one of his muscular forearms beneath her ass supporting her, and she tried to wrap her legs around his hips. The metal brace on her leg dug into her flesh and she groaned with frustration and lowered her legs again, but it didn't seem to bother Quin. His strength astounded her as he held her up without seeming to make any effort. He took and took, turning her smoldering libido into an inferno, but he also gave. Quin's tongue danced with hers and then he ate at her lower lip, sucking it into his mouth, licking and nipping at her flesh.

She was so hot and in such need that she wanted him to strip her down right there and then and touch her. Finally she drew away, gasping in lungfuls of air and staring at him as he lowered her feet to the floor and she removed her arms from around his neck.

"I want you, Eva. We all do. We've been waiting for you to decide what you want. Please don't get our hopes up if you aren't willing to be with all three of us."

"I–I..." *Oh God!* She so wanted to say yes, but wanting wasn't enough for her. She needed more than just lust from them.

"Sugar." Grayson's voice drew her gaze. She hadn't even been aware he was close by. She had been so wrapped up in Pierson and Quin she hadn't heard him approach. He stopped when he was only feet from her and reached out a hand to her. His fingers stroked over her heated cheek, and she closed her eyes at the soft touch. "We won't force you into something if you're not ready. Just think about being in a relationship with us. If you want to be with us it will be exclusively, but you get to make the next move. The decision is yours to make, Eva. We won't pressure you."

Eva gulped audibly and looked to each of them. They looked so eager and yet so vulnerable. She felt a little bad that she wasn't going to give them the answer they wanted to hear, at least not yet.

"I know you want me to say yes," she almost whispered and then paused and drew in a ragged breath. "I can't. Not yet. I need more time."

"You take all the time you need, darlin'. We won't rush you," Pierson said, looking a little sad.

"I'm sorry I can't answer you right now, but I'm not sure how any of this would work. I've only ever had one boyfriend, and it should never have been." She held up her hand when Quin began to speak.

"I haven't finished, Quin," Eva said. "I also want you to know why I feel so cautious." She took a breath. "I have a neighbor back in Sheridan who has been pursuing me rather aggressively over the last two years. We have known each other since we were kids. We grew up together. But Tim has become almost obsessive in his pursuit and made me very wary of men."

"Did he hurt you?" Pierson asked.

"No." She let out a shuddering breath, remembering what he'd done instead. "But he could. Tim served in the military and is pretty beefy. Not as big as you three, but he uses his size in an intimidating way. He's one of the reasons I left Sheridan." She looked between the three of them, watching their expressions anxiously. Gray looked worried, Pierson was frowning almost skeptically, and Quin looked as angry as she'd expected. *You knew this would bring out their protective instincts.*

With a sigh, she concluded, "So my limited experience with the opposite sex has made me…well, cautious, like I said."

"We would never use our height or strength to intimidate you, Eva. Surely you realize that after the last two weeks."

"Yes. I believe you, Quin, but I'm not sure I'm ready to deal with one man, let alone three. Please don't take me the wrong way. I'm not saying no, and I'm sure you realize that I am attracted to all three of you, but I'm just not ready for a relationship. We've only known each other for two weeks." *And I don't understand why you want me.* She knew she couldn't say it aloud, but it was true. The Badons couldn't possibly want someone like her. No one ever did.

"Okay, sugar. We respect your decision and we'll give you the time you need to make a choice. But I want you to promise me something." Gray took her hand in his, caressing the skin on the back with his thumb.

"If I can," she said warily.

"If you decide you want a relationship with us or you need anything from us, and I mean *anything*, you won't hesitate to come and tell us or ask for what you want."

Eva smiled slightly and nodded. "Okay, I promise."

"Thank you, Eva." Gray tugged her against him and gave her a hug. It was so nice to be held by someone. But what would be better was if their bodies were naked with their skin touching, and not just his. *What would it be like to have all three of them touching me?* His voice pulled her mind back to the present. "Now did I hear you say you wanted to stop at the store?"

"You did."

"I'll come with you then. I have a few things I want to pick up."

Eva led the way out to her car and slid into the driver's seat. As she buckled up, Gray got into the passenger side. He was nearly too big for her midsize sedan and had to push the seat all the way back to fit his long legs into her car.

"You're very quiet, sugar. Are you okay?"

"I'm fine, Gray. It's just that I'm feeling a little...overwhelmed right now."

"Talk to me, Eva. Tell me what's on your mind."

Eva concentrated on her driving for a moment, using that task to gather her thoughts. The road was nearly deserted and didn't really need too much of her attention, but she was glad to have something to do. She could feel Gray's eyes on her, and even though she wasn't uncomfortable she just didn't know what she wanted to say or in fact do. So she decided there was nothing like honesty.

"I'm really flattered that you and your brothers are attracted to me, Gray." She directed the car into a free parking space outside the supermarket and shut off the engine and turned to face him. "You've probably figured out by what I've said that I don't have much experience with men. Don't get me wrong. I am attracted to all three of you, but I'm not sure if being in a relationship with all of you is right for me."

"What are your concerns, sugar? Maybe if you talk to me and ask questions we can clear up a few of them."

Eva turned back to stare out the windshield. "I'm not good at sex. My one and only experience proved that to me."

Gray didn't react. She'd been a little afraid that he would agree with her or laugh, but that wasn't Gray. He just watched her thoughtfully and asked, "What made you decide that?"

"My first and only boyfriend was a good friend to me. In fact he was more like a brother. We only ever had each other. He was a nerd and he wasn't a handsome man, but he was one of my best friends. We decided to have sex with each other and it was an utter disaster. Afterward we couldn't even look each other in the eyes. Eventually, we started avoiding each other and then stopped seeing each other completely."

"I'm sorry, Eva," Gray said.

She sighed. "I think we were just so eager to experience things, you know? But we should never have attempted to be physical with each other. I lost one of my closest friends, and I don't want to ever have to go through that again."

"Sweetheart, that wasn't you. You just picked the wrong man to have your first experience with. From what I saw when you kissed Pierson and Quin, you have no worries in that department."

"Oh God." Her cheeks heated and she knew they must be as red as they felt. "I can't believe I did that."

"What? Kissed my brothers?"

She nodded.

"Look at me, Evana," Gray demanded quietly.

Cursing mentally when she complied, Eva tried to turn away again, but once their eyes connected, she couldn't look away.

"I know Quin told you about the ménage relationships in this town from the start. He also told you that we intended to find a woman we were all attracted to and settle down with her. We believe you could be that woman." He reached over and placed a finger on her lips when she opened her mouth, and she closed it again. "What are you so frightened of?"

"I've put up with a lot of derogatory comments for most of my life, Gray. My self-esteem isn't as good as it should be. I have scars on my right hip, the top of my thigh, and even on my knee. I don't like being naked in front of anyone. I have stretch marks from when I grew almost overnight when I was an adolescent, and my boobs are too small. I get stared at all the time, and I wear bars on my leg."

Eva was panting by the time she was finished listing everything that was wrong with her and waited with trepidation for his reply.

Gray smoothed her hair back from her face then stroked his hand over the back of her head and down the length of her tresses. "You have the most beautiful eyes I have ever seen. Your hair literally sparkles when the sun shines down upon it. Did you know you have gold strands threaded in amongst that dark red? Your body is perfect to me and my brothers. I get hard every time you get near me. I love your cute little ass and have to resist bending you over so I can take a bite out of it. The scent you wear wraps around my balls until I ache every time I smell it, and you have the sweetest, most loving and caring personality I have ever seen."

Tears began to fill her eyes. *He sees that in me?*

Gray went on, "In my eyes you are the most picture-perfect, flawless, sensitive, compassionate woman I have ever met. You were made for us, Eva. Everyone has imperfections, sugar, but when somebody cares enough about you, those flaws become invisible."

Eva's tears spilled onto her cheeks. She'd never had anyone besides her mom say anything nice about her. Not even her ex or Tim. Emotion rushed through her, filling her heart with hope and joy and making her fall even more in love with him.

"That's the nicest thing anyone has ever said to me. Thank you."

"Quin and Pierson feel the same way I do, Eva. Please don't make a decision yet. Give yourself time to think over our offer. We will wait for however long you need."

Gray took her face between his hands and wiped her tears away with his thumb. He leaned in close and kissed her on the forehead. "Let's go inside so we can get home. I'll help you with dinner tonight. I'm starving."

"You're always hungry." Eva laughed as he released her and got out of the car.

When she turned back to make sure the locks had engaged she caught sight of a man driving away from them in a dark-colored sedan. The back of his head reminded her of Tim.

Chapter Six

Quin and Pierson closed up shop and drove home in silence. Not until Quin had pulled the truck into the driveway did he voice his thoughts. "I don't like this business about her neighbor."

"At least we know why she is so afraid to live near her mom." Pierson looked pensive, as he had for the entire drive, but then he smiled as he got out of the car. "She's beginning to trust us. She never would have told us about her neighbor if she didn't. Only one thing bothers me…"

Quin shut the driver's-side door and frowned at him. "What?"

"I think she's still left out a hell of a lot about that Tim guy. It has to be a lot worse with her neighbor than she's letting on. No woman I've ever met would pack up and take off unless she was really worried about her safety. I wish she'd tell us what he's done to make her so scared."

Quin unlocked the front door. He hated the idea of Eva being threatened by some asshole who ought to know better. He didn't like her being afraid at all. "Do you think she's scared of us?"

"What? No. Why do you say that?"

Quin realized now that he'd come down hard on her this morning when he found her teetering around on that chair. He stood by his feelings, because she had been putting herself in danger, but he hadn't expressed those feelings well. He was bothered by her words about Tim's size intimidating her.

When Quin didn't answer, Pierson said, "I don't think she's scared of us. We just need to boost her self-esteem and show her that she could have a relationship with us."

"Agreed," Quin said shortly. "She's a passionate, sexy woman and she doesn't even know it."

Pierson grinned. "I can think of a few ways to show her."

Quin could, too. But what if he messed it up the way he had earlier today? Pierson had an easygoing charm that obviously worked on Eva. Sometimes she even flirted with him. She was developing a rapport with Gray, too.

While Quin felt certain of her attraction to him, he feared that another display of temper like the one this morning would scare her off.

No. We won't lose her. He pulled into the driveway of their house, the place that Eva had made a home. When they got out of the car, Pierson said, "Just try and be patient a little longer. She's coming around slowly."

Footsteps alerted him that Gray and Eva were home and he walked toward the doorway in case help was needed to bring in the grocery bags. Her cheeks were flushed, her eyes sparkled, and she looked really happy, the tilt to her lips lighting up her whole face. Evana had never looked more beautiful.

"Let me take those from you, baby." Quin took the bags and carried them to the kitchen counter. "What do you have planned for dinner?"

"Gray and I decided that we'd have steak, baked potatoes, and salad."

"Sounds good, darlin'. Do you want some help?" asked Pierson.

"No, but thanks." Eva walked toward the brewing coffee. "Gray's already volunteered."

"Okay, I'm going to go clean up."

Quin sat on one of the stools at the kitchen counter and watched Gray and Eva as they washed their hands and then began to prepare dinner. He loved having her in their home and didn't want to imagine how empty it would feel if she left.

Eva looked up from chopping vegetables and gave him a frown. He could see she was thinking and wanted to question her but waited patiently instead.

"How do you know you wouldn't get jealous?"

"Of what, baby?"

She took a deep breath and tried again. "If you were in a ménage relationship, how do you know you wouldn't get jealous of your brothers? What if your girlfriend spent more time with one of you and not the others? Wouldn't that cause friction and eventually affect your relationship with each other?"

Quin felt excitement flutter in his belly. If Eva was asking questions, it had to be a good sign. *Doesn't it?*

"Well, for one, we would all take time out to spend with our girl alone, and secondly, we would also have time with her together."

"Yes, but what if she forgot who she was supposed to be having alone time with and went to the wrong brother?"

"It wouldn't matter, Eva. We are all different, and if she needed one of us more than the others at a certain time, then that would be okay. Besides, it's our duty to know whose turn it is to spend time with our woman. She wouldn't have to worry about trying to keep things straight in her head."

"Would she have to play musical beds each night?"

"No, baby." Quin reached for her hand and caressed the back of it with his thumb. "Our wife would have her own room and it would be up to her who she wanted in it. If she just wanted one of us then that's all right. Maybe she would feel the need to have all three of us in her bed or just two. Everything in a ménage relationship revolves around the female. Her wants and needs take precedence over anything else."

"What if she wanted to sleep alone?"

"Then we would let her have the bed to herself. We may not like it, but our woman comes first."

"Hmm." Eva moved her hand away and began chopping again. He wanted to reach over and smooth the frown between her eyes away, but he didn't want to distract her in case she cut herself. The woman was a whiz with a knife. She handled the blade so well, it was almost a blur.

"I have the potatoes in the oven and the steaks marinating," Gray said as he moved close to Eva and wrapped his arms around her waist from behind as she put down the knife. "Where did you learn to wield a knife, sugar?"

"My mom taught me."

"I would love to meet your mother. She sounds like quite a woman," Quin said.

"She is," Eva replied, picking up her coffee and taking a sip. "I'm glad that she found Jack. He's such a nice man, and since she doesn't have to work anymore she's getting time to enjoy life for a change. She should be home soon. I'll have to give her a call."

"What do you mean, Eva?"

"Mom never had time to do anything but work." She sighed. "There were always so many hospital bills."

"Why do you feel guilty about that, Eva?" Gray inquired.

"How did you know...?"

"You have a very expressive face, baby. We often know what you're thinking and feeling."

The expression which crossed her face looked downright horrified.

"Why does that scare you?" asked Quin.

"Uh, I just...I don't like knowing that people know what I'm thinking."

"Don't panic, baby. We didn't see it until we got to know you a little better. A complete stranger wouldn't be able to read you."

"And that's supposed to make me feel better?" she snapped, pulling away from Gray.

"What's going on?" Pierson asked as he entered the room.

"Eva's upset over the fact that we can read her facial expressions and she also feels guilty about her mom having to work to pay for all her medical expenses."

Gray sighed. Quin glanced at him and then at Eva, who was blushing. He realized that maybe Pierson hadn't been asking for such a blunt summary.

Pierson at least took it in stride. He turned to Eva with a look of concern. "Darlin', moms are supposed to take care of their kids. If she hadn't loved you so much, do you think she would have worked two jobs? And we are only able to read some of your expressions since we are just coming to know you. We can't read your mind, Eva."

Quin watched as her tight shoulders seemed to slump with relief. Gray looked at him and cocked an eyebrow, telling him to be careful about what he said.

"Sorry, I guess I'm a bit too sensitive about some subjects." Eva gazed toward Quin.

"No problem, baby. How long before dinner is ready?"

"Approximately thirty minutes."

"Good, that gives me plenty of time to shower and change." Quin skirted the counter, moved in close to Eva, leaned down, and kissed her on the cheek. He straightened once more and headed toward the bathroom without looking back. The grin on his face would probably have made her mad, but he had seen the startled doe-like look in her eyes, and underlying that shock he had seen her desire. That was why she had been so upset when he'd told her they could read her. She was frightened he and his brothers would see how much she wanted them.

Their little Eva was running scared. But not from them. She was frightened of her own feelings.

Chapter Seven

Eva was up and dressed early Saturday morning and was preparing breakfast when Quin entered the kitchen. He came up behind her, wrapped his arms around her waist, and nuzzled her neck.

"You smell good, baby." He kissed her on the cheek and stepped back. "Do you want me to do anything?"

"No, breakfast is just about done."

"Are you looking forward to today?"

She turned and smiled at him after placing the last of the bacon onto the platter. "Yes, I love playing the tourist. Are you sure you want to come with me?"

"Of course we do. We love spending time with you, Eva." Quin took the platter from her hands and carried it to the table just as Gray and Pierson entered the kitchen.

"Something smells good." Gray sniffed the air.

"Sit down and eat. I've made some sandwiches to take with us. I thought we could have a picnic," Eva said.

"That sounds good to me, darlin'." Pierson carried his coffee to the table and sat down.

"How is it that you're all able to take time off? I thought you would have to work on Saturdays, at least in the morning anyway."

"Normally we would, but when we asked you not to schedule any jobs for today it was so we could spend the time with you," Gray answered.

Eva felt warmth penetrating her chest and filling her heart with flutters. They were all so sweet to want to spend time with her when they should be working. Their actions made her feel almost cherished.

Tears pricked the backs of her eyes and she looked down to her plate. She didn't want them to see how affected she was by their kindness. Eva had no idea how long they would want her living with them or working in their garage. Although they had said they were looking to settle down and thought she could be the woman they had been looking for, she was having a hard time believing it. *Why would three tall, sexy, brawny men want me?* As far as she was concerned she had nothing to offer them. Self-doubt reared its ugly head. The only thing she had to offer was her body, and even she knew it wasn't something most men wanted.

"Look at me, Eva," Quin demanded.

Blinking a few times to dispel the moisture in her eyes, she took a slow, deep breath and raised her head. He pinned her with his gaze and she felt like she was drowning in the depths of his eyes.

"Why are you upset?" Quin asked before forking more eggs into his mouth.

"I'm not upset," she lied, placing her silverware on her plate.

"Bullshit." Quin narrowed his eyes at her. "Don't you dare fucking lie to me again!"

"Quin." Gray's voice was low and dangerous. "Calm down."

God, now they're arguing because of me. Eva felt even worse, but Quin did calm down at his brother's warning.

"Tell me why you were on the verge of tears," Quin said. "And this time answer me honestly."

She cleared her throat to make sure it wouldn't squeak or be too raspy with emotion before she answered him. Glancing around at them she saw they had all finished eating and were watching her intently. "Gray's words made me feel special."

"And that made you feel bad?" Gray asked, drawing her eyes toward him. He didn't look happy. His jaw was clenched and the muscles in his jaw ticked.

"No. Yes. I don't know," she whispered and rose from her seat. Eva began clearing the table but kept her eyes averted from them. The room was quiet except for the clank of dishes as she collected them. If she stopped, she could have heard a pin hitting the floor. The tension in the room made it hard for her to breathe.

"We aren't going anywhere until you have given me an answer, little girl."

"No." She didn't expect them to understand. They'd never lived with a disability the way she had. Men as strong and handsome as they were had probably never suffered a moment of self-doubt. Eva turned away and began to rinse the dishes and load the dishwasher.

She jumped when hands landed on her shoulders and spun her around. When she looked up, she mentally cringed at the anger on Quin's face.

Eva's heart sped up, beating hard and fast against her chest. Her breathing escalated and she tried to shrug off his hands. Quin's eyes narrowed and then she shrieked as her world turned upside down. He'd moved so fast she barely saw him as he bent and placed his shoulder into her belly. The next thing she knew she was hanging over his shoulder as he strode from the room.

"Put me down right now," Eva yelled as she struggled.

A hand landed on her ass with a loud *smack*. Oh, he did not just spank me, Eva seethed. There was no way she was letting him get away with that.

"Put me the fuck down." She kicked out her legs and was satisfied when they swung back and landed on his thigh, causing him to grunt. She shrieked when another slap landed on her ass, only this time it was a lot harder than the last.

"Don't you start cussing," Quin snarled. "There is no way I'm letting you sound trashy."

She drew in a breath to let loose a tirade at his double standards, but as she opened her mouth she went flying. Eva's scream was cut off when she landed on something soft and she bounced a few times. Quickly glancing around, she ascertained she was in her bedroom and tried to scramble off the bed. She didn't make it.

A large hand wrapped around her left ankle and another gripped one of the bars of her brace. Quin placed his knees on the bed and virtually threw himself over her, pinning her to the mattress using his whole body. But not once did her hurt her or crush her with his weight.

"Why did Gray's words upset you, Evana?"

Eva didn't want to answer, but she knew by the determined look in Quin's eyes he wasn't going to relent until he had what he wanted.

"He made me feel special," she answered quietly and then glanced away. As soon as she saw Gray and Pierson standing at the end of the bed near the sides she wished she hadn't looked. Gray looked worried, but she could also see that he was hurt. Tears pricked her eyes again. It hadn't been her intention to hurt him at all. She knew what it was like to be hurt over and over again, and because she had hurt him, she felt guilty.

"I'm sorry," Eva said when she looked at Gray.

"Why?" Gray asked. Eva gazed at him for a moment until she realized he wasn't questioning her apology.

"I've never had compliments from anyone but my mother. I don't know how to handle it when people say nice things to me. I don't even know if I believe them."

Gray and Pierson moved around the end of the bed and got up beside her and Quin. Quin shifted until he was sitting between her legs, and even though she wasn't pinned down anymore, she knew by the look in his eye that if she tried to move, he would stop her in an instant.

Pierson reached over, cupped her cheek, and turned her head toward him. "What is going on inside that head of yours, darlin'?"

Eva closed her eyes and tried to gather her thoughts, but a tap to her thigh had them opening again almost immediately.

"Don't close your eyes, baby," Quin commanded. "I'm not letting you close yourself off from us."

She opened her mouth to explain but shut it again, not knowing what to say or how to put her feelings into words.

"Talk to us, damn it!"

"No one ever gives me the time of day. Why do you want to spend time with me?"

"Why do you think?" Gray snapped.

She'd never heard that tone from Gray before, and it sent shards of pain into her chest. Eva hated it when people got angry with her, but it hurt more that she had caused these three men to be unhappy. She shook her head and looked up at the ceiling.

"You know damn well that we are all attracted to you, Eva. Why wouldn't we want to spend time with you and give you compliments?"

"Because they're not true," she wailed. "You say nice things to me but I know you don't really mean them. Why would you want to have a relationship with boring ole me when you could have your pick of any woman you wanted?"

"You think we're lying?" Quin asked incredulously. "Why would we do that?"

"Did you think I was lying in the car yesterday when I told you how beautiful you were?" Gray glared at her with narrowed eyes.

Eva's impulse was to nod, but it wasn't true. She had believed him. She shook her head instead.

"How many boyfriends have you had, darlin'?" Pierson queried.

Since she had no idea why that was relevant she just gawked at him.

"Answer the question, Eva."

"One."

"Tell us about your boyfriend."

"I've already told you about him."

"How long did you go out with him?"

"Six months."

"What sort of things did you do together?"

"We just hung out."

"Okay, but where did you hang out?" Pierson helped her to sit up when she tried to scoot up the bed. He made sure pillows were mounded behind her before she leaned back.

"The campus library, mostly."

"Did this guy ever take you out dancing or to dinner and the movies?"

"No."

"So you were dating but never went on dates." Gray moved up and leaned against the headboard next to her.

"I guess."

"Was he ashamed of you?" Quin questioned.

Eva felt her cheeks heat but shook her head no, but as she thought about her ex's behavior she began to realize that he had been ashamed to be seen with her anywhere other than at the college.

"I didn't think so at the time, but now that I think back, yes, I believe he was."

"Tell us about Tim."

Adrenaline pumped through her system, causing her to want to flee. Just someone mentioning that asshole's name caused her to panic.

"What did he do to you, sugar?" Gray reached over and clasped her hand in his. His fingers stroked over her skin until the pad of his finger rested on her inner wrist.

"He hasn't done anything other than ask me out."

"I don't believe you, Eva." Quin reached out and gripped her chin between thumb and finger so she couldn't look away from him. "Tell us why he frightens you."

"I can't prove anything. I've never seen him do anything wrong."

"All right then. Tell us what you suspect he has done."

Eva licked her dry lips and thought over all the creepy things she suspected Tim of. "I think he's been in my bedroom."

"What makes you think that?" Pierson asked in a calm voice.

"Some of my panties and bras have gone missing."

"Son of a..." Quin cut off his own curse. "You think he took them?"

"Yes."

"Tell us the rest, Eva." Gray's grip on her hand firmed.

"When he sees me, he looks at me like he knows what I'm wearing beneath my clothes."

"Is that it?"

"No," she sighed, knowing the three Badon brothers weren't going to quit until she'd revealed all. "He's left things for me."

"What type of things?"

"I'd find a rose on my pillow when I woke up in the morning and a couple of times he's left toys. The house is always locked up at night. With just mom and I being on our own for so long, we became almost obsessive about securing the house. I think Tim may have found the key my mom gave his. He's been coming into my bedroom while I'm sleeping." She shuddered.

"Toys?" Quin raised an eyebrow. "What type of toys?"

"Once I found a vibrator and another time I found a small box. When I opened it there were two balls in it and they were connected by a string. I have no idea what they are but I just know whatever the message is it can't be good."

"Ben Wa balls," Gray growled.

"What?"

"Never mind," Quin said. "Is that it?"

"No."

"Shit! Tell us the rest."

"I woke up to find a butt plug on my spare pillow with instructions and a bottle of lubricant next to it."

"Fuck. This guy is sick." Gray scowled at her. "Why didn't you call the cops? You could have had him charged with breaking and entering as well as stalking."

"I can't. His mom is my mom's best friend. It would devastate them both."

"I would rather them be devastated than have you in danger, baby," Quin said. "He's a sick fuck. Have you thought that if he doesn't get you to go out with him he could end up raping you?"

"I told you I don't even know if it is Tim who's breaking in and leaving those things." *I know damn well it's him, but I can't prove it and I don't want to hurt his mother. She is such a sweet, gentle woman. It would devastate her to find out what her only son has been doing.* "I've never heard him or caught him. I don't know how he does it. He must be really quiet."

"I'd love to confront this bastard and pound on him for scaring you," Gray said in a growly voice.

"Tim's just as big as you are. You would end up killing each other."

"Just because he's big doesn't mean he has any muscle." Quin scrubbed a hand over his face.

"He does. Tim was in the army." She hesitated and then went on, "That's not all."

"What else is going on, baby?" Quin asked.

"I'm worried that Tim may have followed me."

"What makes you think he knows where you are?" Gray picked up her hand and threaded his fingers with hers.

Eva drew in a shaky breath. "I thought I saw him a couple of times." She shifted in her seat. "I can't be sure though, because both times I only saw the back of his head."

"Okay," Quin said. "Never discount a gut instinct. If you think this guy has followed you, then we'll look into it. And that settles it. You'll just have to stay here. There is no way I'm letting you go back home. You'd be in danger."

"Excuse me?" Eva asked.

"You heard me, baby. Get used to the idea. Besides, you don't want to leave. All that stuff before was because you are scared about your feelings for us. Do you honestly think we don't know you are beginning to care for us, Eva? Well, let me tell you something, sweetheart. We care for you, too, and there is no way in hell we're letting you get away." Quin got up off the bed and headed toward the bedroom door. "Now move your ass, baby, we have some sightseeing to do."

Eva's mouth gaped open as she watched Quin leave without a backward glance. Gray released her hand and kissed her on the cheek. "You're special, sugar, and I know you don't realize how much, but we are going to make you believe it."

She was still in shock with the way Quin had just blurted out that they cared for her. She wanted to jump off the bed and run after him and throw herself at them, but she wasn't that brave. It filled her with hope that they didn't feel any pity toward her and honestly had feelings for her.

When Pierson took her face between his hands and planted a light but sweetly emotional kiss on her lips moisture pricked the backs of her eyes. "We could have everything together, darlin'. Don't push us away before we even have the chance to find out."

Chapter Eight

Gray enjoyed taking the river cruise with Eva and his brothers. She had taken in all the sights and obviously loved the tranquility of water because she was more relaxed than he had ever seen her before. There had been a few exhilarating moments as they had shot various rapids on the tour. Though Eva had clutched at whoever of them was nearest, she had laughed the whole time. Today she seemed to have more vitality, and her cheeks were still pink from the experience and the fresh air.

Quin turned off the highway into some picnic grounds they had found online, and Gray helped Eva from the truck while Pierson grabbed the basket and blanket they had stowed in the back. Gray wondered what time Eva had woken up to have made all the food for their picnic and then their breakfast. She had risen before any of them, as she usually did, and took such good care of them that he wanted her in their house permanently. But not just because of her nurturing side or the sexual chemistry between all of them. Although it had only literally been weeks since they had met Eva, Gray was in love with her and he knew his brothers were as well. He wanted to pull her into his arms and kiss her until neither of them could breathe. He wanted to strip her down and love on her body with his hands and mouth until she was writhing with pleasure, and then he would sink balls-deep into her tight, wet pussy.

Adjusting his hard, aching cock, he watched the gentle sway of her hips as she moved. He didn't see the slight limp she walked with or the bars on her leg. All he saw was the woman of his dreams. Quin and Pierson had the picnic area set up in minutes. Moving in closer to

Eva, Gray took her hand and helped her down to the blanket. Together they passed out the food. Their woman was a veritable marvel in the kitchen, and he sighed after he inhaled the aroma of cooked chicken, potato salad, and a tossed salad. He also caught the scent of something sweet.

"What time did you get up, sugar?" Gray queried.

"Um, around five, I think."

"As much as we appreciate the time and effort you've put into this picnic," Quin said, "we don't want you running yourself ragged, baby. This is your day off, too. We could have just gone to the mall and bought food or taken you out for lunch."

"Speak for yourself," Pierson piped up. "Eva, this is all delicious. If you want to cook, I for one welcome every mouthful you've prepared."

"I didn't mean I don't appreciate what she's done, Pierson." Quin scowled at his brother. "But Eva needs rest, too."

"I…"

"Guys," Eva interrupted, "please don't argue. I know what you meant, Quin, but I'm used to getting up early and I'm sure you've all realized how much I love to cook."

"You are getting dark smudges beneath your eyes, darlin'." Pierson handed out the plastic cutlery and began to load his plate with food. "We are worried about you. Are you still having trouble sleeping?"

Since Gray was sitting next to Eva, he heard her draw in a long breath, even though he knew she was trying to hide that fact. He turned toward her and saw an expression he'd never seen on her face before and couldn't quite discern what it was.

"I'm fine."

Gray realized she wasn't fine at all and hoped she would open up more with them but decided to see if she would trust them with whatever was worrying her without pushing her. Trust worked both ways, and he needed her to trust him and his brothers without being too commanding. He could be just as determined and dominant as Quin, but this time he felt the need to let Eva open up on her own terms. Quin obviously wasn't as patient.

"You aren't fine, baby. Tell us why you are having trouble sleeping."

"I said I'm fine, Quin." Eva glared at his brother where he sat on the blanket across from her. "Just leave it alone, okay?"

Gray looked from Quin to Eva and back again. Quin's eyes narrowed into slits and he glared at Eva with frustration. Eva stuck her chin out toward his sibling, and he could see if he or Pierson didn't butt in and change the subject, a fight would result.

"You make the best food, Eva. It all tastes delicious. Thank you, sugar."

"You're welcome," Eva replied and concentrated on her food. The silence and tension was so thick Gray swore he could have cut it with one of the plastic knives brought for their picnic.

"Stop changing the damn subject," Quin snapped. His words were directed at Gray, but his eyes were still on Eva. "Damn it, Eva, we want to be able to help you. If you won't talk to us, how the hell are we supposed to know what is going on with you?"

"Maybe you aren't," Eva replied vehemently.

"You aren't happy with us, are you, darlin'?" Pierson voiced the one question Gray would never have had the guts to ask. And from the look Quin shot toward his brother, he wasn't too happy either.

"I'm not sad," Eva replied, and Gray let go of the breath he hadn't known he was holding until then.

"What is going on in that beautiful head of yours, sugar? We don't mean to pry, but your welfare and health mean a lot to us."

Gray placed his plate on the rug and reached out to gently caress her face with the tip of a finger. When Eva looked up at him, he could see how forlorn she felt. He wanted to pluck her off the rug, pull her onto his lap, and envelop her in his arms, but he also needed her to tell them why she was so sad.

"You only feel sorry for me," Eva blurted and her cheeks slowly turned pink.

"Eva, we don't feel pity for you." Gray frowned. "Why would you even think that?"

"Then why are you so worried about how much sleep I get, as if I were an invalid? Just because I'm disabled doesn't mean I'm a delicate flower." Eva was as red as the tomato on her plate by now. "I don't appreciate being babied. That's why you waited weeks to kiss me, isn't it? I know you aren't the type of men to wait around for what you want. You're scared I can't handle you. And it's what everyone else always feels toward me."

Gray was stunned. Eva's sassy side had made an appearance, and he couldn't believe how much he'd misread her. But it made sense— Eva knew she had been running from her feelings for them, and now she wanted them but was too scared to come out and say it.

"Eat your food," Quin commanded and pointed toward her plate. "When you're done we are going to talk about your insecurities."

The rest of the meal was eaten in tense silence. Gray kept his head down as he ate to hide his smile. He knew Quin was just biding his time, planning how to show Eva that they knew she could indeed handle them.

Once everyone was done, Gray and Pierson began to clear away the remnants of their picnic.

"Come here, Eva," Quin demanded.

Eva eyed his outstretched hand and shook her head and then rose to her feet.

"I'm going for a walk," she stated, turned, and began to walk away.

Gray looked at Quin and saw he had planned on baiting Eva. There was a decided sparkle in his brother's eyes and the knowledge that Eva would balk at another command from Quin. His brother stood up and had snagged Eva around the waist before she had taken more than five steps.

"You will do as I say when I tell you to do something." Quin growled through clenched teeth. "This is your only warning, baby. The next time you go over my knee."

"Don't you dare threaten me, you asshole."

"Oh, it wasn't a threat, Eva. If I decide you're going over my knee, you will, and you'll like it. That's a promise. And I know I have already told you to watch that mouth. You are going to get a spanking, so next time you want to cuss, you'll think about it before you even speak."

Quin lifted Eva up into his arms. One arm slid to her knees and the other wrapped under her shoulders. Eva shrieked and wriggled, trying to get free, but Gray knew that wasn't about to happen.

"Stop!" Quin ordered. "I don't want you hurting yourself."

"Screw you!"

"Oh, we'll get to that eventually, baby, and that is also a promise."

Quin knelt on the blanket but kept one leg raised with his foot flat on the ground. With expert ease he quickly but carefully tipped Eva up and over his knee, her stomach across his thigh.

"Let me go. What the hell do you think you're doing?" Eva yelled.

Gray moved across the rug and grasped her hands and stretched them out so she couldn't harm herself trying to get away from Quin. He saw Pierson move to her feet and clasp her ankles in his hands.

"Why are you helping him?" Eva asked angrily. "You should be helping me get away."

"Why would I help you get away?" Gray brought her hands together so he could hold them. "I think Quin's right."

She looked even more outraged. "You think that I should be spanked?"

"No. I think you're going to like it. And I'm going to like watching."

Eva stared at him, her expression stunned. Before she could continue arguing, as Gray had no doubt she would, Quin caressed his palm over Eva's denim-clad bottom, and her struggling stopped. She drew in a gasp and then tipped her head to the side, trying to see Quin.

The first smack to land wasn't hard, but it did make a lot of noise as Quin had cupped his hand. Eva squeaked, but that was the only sound she made and then she tried to hide her face again. Her head hung down and her hair covered her cheeks.

"Get her jeans off." The danger of being caught out in the open only seemed to add an exciting element to the air.

Gray expected Eva to protest, but again she didn't speak. He bent down slightly, trying to see her expression, but her hair was in the way. With a gentle hand, he swept her hair over one shoulder and caught her nibbling on her lower lip. Her cheeks were flushed and her eyes were closed.

Pierson pulled Eva's jeans down to midthigh but kept her panties on. The second smack landed on her satin-clad backside, and Eva let out a breathy sigh. Quin landed ten smacks in all, making sure not to hit the same place twice and treating both of her buttocks evenly. By the time he had finished Eva was moaning and thrusting her hips up at his brother, demanding more.

"Does this feel like we pity you, Eva?" Quin smoothed his hand over her butt, waiting for an answer. When she didn't, Quin slipped a thumb beneath the elastic of her panties and slowly drew them down. "I'll bet you're wet, aren't you, baby?"

Gray wasn't certain if Quin expected an answer. He watched as her pink cheeks came into view. His brother pushed the little scrap of material down until all of her beautiful ass was exposed. His hand slid between her legs.

"Oh, you are soaked, baby. Did you enjoy your spanking?"

"Yes," Eva moaned.

Gray could see Quin's forearm flexing and moving and wanted to watch what his brother was doing to their woman. He released her hands and placed them palms down on the rug. "Leave your hands where they are, sugar. I don't want you to hit your head on the ground if you wriggle around too much."

Rising to his feet, Gray moved around Eva's backside and sat on the rug next to Quin. He was right where he needed to be to see what his brother was doing to Eva as Pierson had spread her legs as wide as he could with her jeans bunched at her knees.

Eva's pussy was so wet and creamy he wanted to get between her splayed thighs and lick her pretty little cunt, but he didn't want to interrupt what Quin was doing to her as she seemed to like it.

"You are so hot, wet, and tight," Quin rasped as he pumped a finger in and out of Eva's pussy. "We want to make you feel good, baby. Will you let us?"

"Please." Eva moaned.

"Please what, darlin'?" Pierson questioned.

"I want you." She bucked her hips up. "I want all of you."

Quin removed his hand from between her legs, grasped her ribs, and turned her over while helping her to sit upright on the rug. "That's all we needed to hear, baby," he said and looked to him and Pierson. "Get her clothes off."

Pierson unhooked the cuff at her knee and then pulled both her boots and socks from her feet. Once they were gone, he helped remove her jeans and panties while Quin undid three buttons on her shirt and then lifted it up and over her head. Next he unclasped her black lace bra and gently lowered her to the blanket until she was lying on her back.

She was absolutely perfect in Gray's eyes. Her red hair looked like it was on fire as it shimmered in the afternoon sunlight, causing the gold threads through her tresses to stand out even more. Eva's green eyes were half-closed. She would have looked dazed but for the passionate glow as she stared at all three of them. Her naturally pink lips were parted, gasping in pants of air.

Never had he seen a more beautiful sight or a more innocently sexy woman. Her breasts were lush and tipped with dusky rose areolas and her hard nipples stood up from the glorious globes. Although she wasn't skinny in that wafer-thin model way, Eva was nowhere near to being called fat. Her rib cage, encased in milky-white skin, tapered to her slim waist, which then gently flared out to her perfect hips. She had long, shapely thighs and calves, and the trimmed hair on her mound nearly exactly matched the hair on her head, including the threads of gold.

Gray groaned as the dappled sunlight caressed her body through the trees. Slowly, almost as if in a dream, he knelt down next to her and then he lay down on his side close to her. Leaning over, he lightly kissed her lips and traced them with the tip of his tongue. Eva surprised him by reaching up, grabbing handfuls of his hair, and pulling his lips tighter against hers. He moaned, tilted his head for a better angle, and kissed her with a deep hunger.

His tongue pushed into her mouth, and he twined it with hers and then tasted every inch of her moist cavern. The little whimpering sounds Eva made as Gray made love to her mouth only enhanced the desire he felt for her. When he withdrew, they were both panting heavily. Movement on her other side caught his attention, and he watched Pierson get down on the rug next to her. He looked down her body and saw Quin moving in between her lax legs, pushing them wider as he laid belly down on the blanket, his mouth hovering over her mound.

Gray cupped a breast, testing the weight, and then kneaded the soft flesh with his palm and fingers. Just as Quin lowered his head and took his first taste of their woman, Gray shifted his thumb and rasped it over her turgid nipple. Eva cried out and arched her neck while pushing her chest forward and wriggling her hips.

He wanted to make love with Evana right this instant and knew his brothers wanted the same, but he was less sure that Eva knew what she was asking for. She might want them just as much, but despite what she'd said, Gray couldn't stop guiltily wondering if she could handle them.

Chapter Nine

Eva couldn't believe how turned on she was after having her ass spanked. Throughout the spanking, cream leaked from her pussy onto her panties, and they were so wet they were ineffectual in containing her desire. Her thighs were damp and her pussy felt swollen with need. One moment Quin had been ordering his brothers to strip off her clothes, and the next she was laid out on the picnic blanket like a feast.

Gray leaned over and kissed her hungrily. His tongue pushed into her mouth and explored. Eva knew she would never be able to get enough of him. She knew that other people wouldn't approve of her being naked before three men, but she melted against Gray as he kissed her. She couldn't fight anymore. Eva had been drawn to them from the start, and they had gradually worked their way into her heart. She didn't want to need them or feel anything for them, but she did, and it scared the bejesus out of her.

Her breath hitched when Gray cupped her breast and began to massage it, and then a long groan emerged from her throat when he flicked his thumb across her nipple. When large, warm hands pushed against her thighs, she spread them readily and nearly screamed as a wet tongue licked her from clit to pussy hole and back again. Another mouth sucked at her other nipple and Eva thought she would die from pleasure. Never would she have imagined that three men would be giving her so much bliss at the same time.

The mouth on her pussy lifted, causing Eva to cry out with frustration.

"You taste so damn sweet, baby. I can't get enough of you."

The deep rumble of Quin's voice sent another shiver coursing up her spine. She whimpered as his tongue licked from her clit down through her drenched folds and thrust into her pussy. He didn't stop there for long though. His tongue caressed her perineum and then he lapped over the sensitive skin of her ass.

"What…" was all Eva could manage to gasp as that slick tongue laved her back entrance over and over again.

"Do you like having your ass licked, darlin'?"

Eva didn't want to answer. She was too embarrassed at feeling pleasure from such an erotically sinful deed, but with each carnal slide of Quin's tongue, that embarrassment waned and turned to desire for more.

"Answer the question, sugar," Gray demanded, pinching her nipple between thumb and finger. The erotic pain sent shards of pleasure zinging straight down to her pussy.

"I–I…Yes."

"Good girl." Quin lifted his head, giving her a heated stare. "I would have known if you lied to me, Eva."

While he kept his gaze pinned to hers, Quin slowly pushed a finger into her vagina. Eva tried to hold in the groan of bliss bubbling up from her chest, but when both Pierson and Gray nibbled on her nipples and scraped their teeth over her sensitive nubs, the groan turned to a gasp and then a whimper of need. Her whole body was on fire and felt like it was about to snap. Then Quin added another finger to her pussy and laved his tongue over her clit with rapid flicks. Warmth permeated her body, centering in her womb and spreading out, causing her toes to curl. He opened his mouth over her engorged nub, sucked it in between his lips, and suckled on her button.

The tension which had slowly been gathering in her body came to a precipice and snapped. Eva screamed as great orgasmic waves of nirvana washed over her, making her body shake, jerk, and shudder. She moaned as Quin removed his fingers from her pussy. Through heavy eyelids, she watched as he licked them clean. It was such an erotic, carnal sight that her just-sated libido quivered with awakening renewal.

Quin rose to his feet, pulled his T-shirt up over his head, and threw it carelessly aside. His hands went to his belt and the fastenings of his jeans. Next, his thumbs hooked into the waist of the denim and pushed them and his underwear down over his hips. She drew in a ragged breath as she eyed his monster cock. She should have known he would be built proportionately there since he was such a big man. Eva closed her legs and squeezed them together, doubting that his large appendage would fit inside her body, but all thoughts fled when Quin turned to his side and bent over. His ass was just as muscular as the rest of him and she wanted to grip his flesh to test the beefy resistance she knew she would feel when she dug her fingers into his cheeks. When he stood once more, she realized he had removed his boots so he could get his jeans and boxers off. The man was the epitome of masculinity, and she wanted to touch every hard, muscled inch of him.

Movement in her peripheral vision caught her attention and she turned to see Gray had removed his shirt but still had his jeans on. On her other side, Pierson was also displaying his brawny chest, shoulders, arms, and torso. All three of the Badons were powerfully built and drool worthy and would put most of the men in her hometown to shame.

Quin lowered himself to his knees and leaned over her, caging her with his body. He was resting on his arms, which were beside her shoulders, and his knees were outside her thighs, but he wasn't touching her anywhere. The air in her lungs expelled with a rush and she gasped for another breath as Quin leaned down until their mouths were only inches apart.

"I want to make love to you, Eva." Quin's moist breath brushed over her lips, causing gooseflesh to rise up over her skin and her pussy to leak out more cream. "Tell me now if you don't want me."

Eva couldn't deny him. She had craved each man's touch since nearly the beginning. Now that she had the chance to experience their touch, their bodies loving her, there was no way she was going to refuse them. She wanted them just as much as they seemed to want her, and she never had been a hypocrite.

"I'll take that as a yes."

Quin's mouth plundered hers. He swept his tongue inside, and when she tasted her essence on his tongue, she whimpered at the eroticism of such a carnal act. When his body lowered onto hers and he covered her totally, his hard cock slipping between her legs, she shifted and tried to give him better access. Without removing his mouth from hers, Quin maneuvered until his legs were inside her splayed thighs and once more depressed her into the blanket beneath. Finally he lifted his head and stared down at her with such heat and hunger, she gasped.

"I can't wait anymore, Eva," Quin said in a deep voice.

He kept his eyes on hers. Nudging her thighs apart even more, he braced his weight on one arm and with his free hand guided his hard shaft to her pussy. Eva bucked her hips upward, trying to get him inside with a desperation she never imagined she could feel. He held still. Her groan of intense expectation and frustration turned to a mewl of delight as he slowly pushed in.

He was so wide Eva felt her delicate, wet flesh parting to permit him entrance. With a slight thrust the head of his cock popped through her sensitive tissue and he held still.

"You are so fucking tight and wet, baby, and you feel so damn good," Quin rasped.

She could see sweat forming on his brow and knew then that he was taking things slow for her. Her heart clenched and warmth suffused her chest knowing that he was taking such good care of her. With his cock seated, he placed his hand back on the ground next to her shoulder. Quin's face was tense and twisted with pleasure and he rocked forward and back, gaining more depth in her pussy. At first her muscles resisted, but when the slight erotic burn turned to bliss, she whimpered and reached for his hips. By the time Quin's cock was buried in her pussy balls-deep, Eva felt as if she was on the very edge of climax once more.

He moved again. This time he sat back on his haunches between her legs, hooked her limbs over the crooks of his elbows, and then shifted over her with his arms once more, leaning on the blanket next to her shoulders. Folded in half like this, she felt every inch of him as he slid deeper inside her than before. As he began to move his hips, dragging and pushing his hard shaft in and out of her pussy, he increased the pace. Every breath that left her mouth sounded like a sob, and even though she tried to hold the sounds back, it was impossible.

Tension began to form along her inner walls, coiling the muscles tighter and tighter and tighter. The more Quin moved, the faster he thrust until the sound of their flesh slapping together along with their panting were the only things she could hear.

With each forward pump of his hips, his balls slapped against her damp ass and enhanced her pleasure. Fingers plucked both her nipples at the same time, and although she knew Pierson and Gray were both touching her and she wanted to look at them, she couldn't look away from Quin. There was so much emotion in his eyes that Eva found herself mesmerized. His mouth twisted as if in pain and then he slammed into her hard and fast, repeating the action again and again. With each thrust, he twisted his hips as his pelvis met hers so that his pubic bone brushed against her sensitive clit.

The desire coursing through her escalated, sending liquid warmth traversing through her womb, deep into her pussy, and down her legs. Her clit throbbed and twitched. Eva arched her neck, closed her eyes, and screamed as she reached ecstasy.

In quick succession her pussy clenched down hard and released on the thick cock shuttling in and out of her vagina, again and again and again. She couldn't seem to get enough air into her lungs as rapture tore her body apart and then seemed to put her back together again. Just as the contractions and shivers began to wane, Quin's fingers applied pressure to her clit and squeezed gently. As she cried out, Eva's voice sounded hoarse even to her ears, her body spasming when another orgasm washed over her. Fluid rushed from her sex, coating her ass cheeks and no doubt Quin, too. Only vaguely aware of Quin roaring his completion, she felt his cock jerk inside her and warmth spewed into her channel.

As her body began to cool, she became aware of Quin slumped down over her. His face was buried against her neck and her arms were wrapped around his shoulders. She stroked her palms up and down his back, relishing his warm, slick, sweaty skin beneath her fingers. Her pussy gave the occasional shudder and twitch until finally her internal muscles stilled. Quin pressed up to his elbows and brushed her damp hair back from her face.

"Are you all right, baby?"

"Yeah," Eva sighed.

"I didn't hurt you, did I?"

"No."

"Good." Quin kissed her lips and then rolled them both onto their sides. Her back brushed against Gray and she turned her head to see him watching her with a wistful smile. She smiled back and lifted her arm back toward him. He lay down behind her and cuddled up close to her back. Looking over Quin's shoulder, she reached out to Pierson and held his hand when he took hers.

In that moment, with Quin's softening cock still inside her and his arms wrapped around her, Gray cuddling her back, and Pierson's hand in her own, she felt loved, cherished, and wanted for who she was, bum hip and all, for the first time in her life.

Sighing with contentment, she lowered her head back onto Quin's bicep and let her eyes close. She was surrounded by their warm bodies and totally satiated with the sun streaming down through the trees and touching her face. Eva felt like she was in love for the first time in her life.

She smiled and relished the closeness she felt with them until she was in danger of falling asleep. Although she was sandwiched between two men, the sun was going down and the air was cooling off. Since she was naked, she was beginning to feel chilled.

Quin's flaccid cock had slipped from her body, and she was feeling a little sticky. Sighing with resignation, she kissed his lips and then pushed against his chest, levering herself into a sitting position.

"Wait, Eva," Quin said and turned away to rummage in the picnic basket. He pulled out several paper napkins and gently wiped between her thighs and then began to dress.

Not used to such caring but intimate actions, she felt her cheeks heat as she blushed and quickly reached for her clothes. Gray handed Eva her panties since they had been just out of reach and Pierson handed over her bra. After she was dressed and all their picnic things were cleared away, they all made their way back to the truck. Quin carried the basket and blanket while Pierson and Gray each held her hands. When they reached the truck she stood back and watched the men secure everything.

They were standing in a circle of sunlight, and their hair and bodies seemed to glow. Her breath caught in her throat. To Eva it felt like God approved of her relationship with the three Badon brothers and gave His blessing.

Chapter Ten

Pierson wrapped an arm around Eva's shoulders and pulled her against his side as her eyelids slid closed. He inhaled her clean, womanly scent and tried to shift and relieve the ache in his cock without disturbing her. He couldn't get the vision of her and Quin making love in the open air out of his mind, no matter how hard he tried.

The image of her as she was in the throes of climax would be forever etched into his heart and mind. She had looked so sweet and innocent yet sexy and wanton at the same time. Eva had looked surprised the first time she climaxed and he wondered if her previous boyfriend had ever taken the time to learn her body and discover the woman inside her. From what she had told him and his brothers about her ex, Pierson didn't think so. Maybe she'd never had an orgasm from a man before. If not, then that would explain the bewilderment that crossed her face right before she reached orgasm. Once she had come down from her first climactic high, she had looked at them all with hunger and he knew she hadn't even been aware of how much she was letting them see.

He'd worked out how their beautiful woman thought after the last couple of weeks. Evana Woodridge liked to think she didn't display her emotions for all to see. She liked to be in control of her life and keep people at arm's length. She was the love of his life, but he didn't think she was ready to hear how much she meant to him even if she needed to.

Quin slowed the truck and rolled to a stop close to the house. Eva didn't even stir. Pierson handed Eva off to Gray while Quin opened the door to the house.

Pierson followed Gray to Eva's room and watched his brother lay their woman on her bed. He helped remove her shoes, and then the two of them placed her under the covers and pulled them up. He smiled over at Gray when she sighed in her sleep and rolled over onto her side. As she clutched the pillow, he heard her whisper all three of their names.

Back downstairs, he and his brothers made some stew. Pierson put on a pot of coffee and it had just finished brewing when a high-pitched feminine cry rent the air. Pierson was on his feet and running before thought even entered his head. The heavy footsteps reverberating behind him let him know Quin and Gray followed.

Pierson barged through Eva's bedroom door, his eyes searching her out. She was lying on the bed, but instead of finding her in the throes of a nightmare, he saw that Eva had pushed the quilt down and was writhing in pain, her hands gripping the lower half of her right leg. Tears were streaming down her face, which was contorted with agony.

"Fuck," Quin snapped. "Get the massage oil, liniment, and heat packs."

Gray turned toward their bathroom, where Quin had insisted they have the necessary supplies on hand for just this purpose. Pierson moved toward the bed and gently pried her hands from her leg.

"Let go, darlin'." He spoke calmly, hoping his low, even voice would help calm her. "We need to get your jeans off so we can help you."

Eva removed her hands from her leg and clutched at the sheet below her body. Pierson could tell she was trying to stay still so they could help her, but she was having a lot of trouble. Her body twitched and jerked in pain. Finally with Quin's help they got her jeans and socks off and Gray reappeared with the massage oil.

Pierson crawled onto the bed above and behind Eva, pushing pillows behind his back. Once settled he grasped her under the arms and pulled her into the *V* of his legs. Wrapping his arms around her chest, beneath her breasts, he spoke quietly into her ear, trying to calm her down.

"Shh, darlin', try and relax. Let Quin and Gray work those nasty kinks out for you."

Pierson hated that Eva was in such pain. Every muscle in her body was tense and taut, and she was sobbing and whimpering as tears streamed down her face. Lavender and vanilla permeated the air as Gray rubbed his oil-slicked hands together, warming the liquid, and then his brother began to work on Eva's right leg while Quin began at her foot.

He could see her toes curling under as the muscles in her foot and leg spasmed, and he knew she must be hurting a lot. She gave a cry as Gray's fingers worked into the muscles in her calf, pushing hard and deep. Pierson just wished he could take her pain away and suffer it himself. He hated that Eva was going through so much discomfort and tried to help the only way he could think of. Smoothing his hands up and down her arms and massaging her shoulders, he crooned nonsensical noises, trying to take her mind from her suffering.

"Shit," Gray snapped. "Her muscles are too far gone. I can't get them to let go."

"Heat," Eva sobbed.

"I'll run a bath." Quin frowned at Eva as she arched when another bout of torment assailed her.

"Hurry," Pierson growled.

"I know," Quin called back over his shoulder. "I hate seeing her in such agony, too."

Pierson sighed with relief when he heard water running in the tub, but Gray didn't let up on kneading her leg as he tried to get her muscles to stop spasming. Before long Quin called from the other room, "Bring her in."

Pierson shifted out from behind Eva, and when he had his feet on the floor, he bent over the bed, scooped her up into his arms, and carried her to the bathroom. He lowered her into the water, careless of the fact that she still had on her shirt, bra, and panties. Once he let her go, he began to strip off. The tub was a large spa bath, more than capable of holding all of them without being cramped. When he was naked he climbed into the tub and pulled her onto his lap. Quin and Gray quickly removed their clothes and hopped in with them.

Another cry emerged from her mouth, and her whole body arched with distress. Wrapping his arms around her waist, he tried to hold her steady while Quin and Gray began to work on her again. The water was slick with oil, which made it easier for his brothers to massage her skin and knead her contracting muscles.

After what seemed like an interminable amount of time, Eva slumped against him. Her body was tired from fighting the convulsive muscles for so long. The muscles in her leg had stopped spasming, thank God. Sighing with relief that Eva was no longer in pain, he pulled her in tight against his chest and she huffed out a breath, resting her head on his shoulder.

"Are you okay, baby?" Quin asked, his hands and fingers still working on her lower leg.

"Yeah," Eva said on an exhale. "Thank you all for helping me. I'm sorry to be such a bother."

"Don't," Gray bit out then must have realized he sounded angry. "Sorry. You're no bother, Eva. We just hate it that you have to suffer so much. Is there anything that can be done to stop you from having these debilitating cramps?"

"No." Eva rubbed her cheek against Pierson's pectorals. "There is nothing to be done. All I can do is keep taking magnesium tablets and try not to strain my muscles too much."

"Shit," Quin growled. "We pushed you too hard today, didn't we?"

"No!" Eva pressed against his chest and sat up straight. "It has nothing to do with what I did today. Sometimes there is no rhyme or reason to what brings the cramps on."

"Are you sure, darlin'?" Pierson asked, still uncertain he and his brothers hadn't contributed to her pain.

"Yeah, I'm sure."

"Let's get you out of the tub, baby," Quin said and offered her a hand after he stood. "You must be feeling hungry after such a long day."

Eva took his hand and let him help her from the bath. The three of them dried her off and dressed her. After Pierson pulled his clothes back on, he grasped her hand and led Eva toward the kitchen.

"What can I do to help?" Eva asked when he checked and stirred their dinner.

"Just sit down and relax, darlin'."

Quin and Gray entered the kitchen and began to get out bowls, silverware, and a wineglass. Then they grabbed three beers and opened a bottle of wine.

"Drink," Quin commanded, handing her the full glass. "The alcohol will help you to relax even more."

"I don't usually…"

"Do as you're told, baby. I want you nice and calm."

Eva gave him an irritated look but sipped her wine.

Pierson brought the pot of stew to the table and placed it on a pot holder. After taking his seat opposite her he took her bowl from Gray's hand and filled it with food. He watched her intently as they all began to eat, and with each mouthful she took, she seemed to become even more tense.

What the hell is going on with you, darlin'? Are you embarrassed about this afternoon? Are you having second thoughts about being with all of us? Are you still in pain? God, I just want to hold you and love you for the rest of our lives. He watched as she began to push her food around her bowl instead of eat it. She'd hardly made a dent in her meal, and Pierson was beginning to get really worried.

"That's it!" Quin exploded. "We have had enough of you shutting us out, Eva. You'd better start talking and tell us what is going on in that pretty little head of yours."

Dammit, Quin. Pierson wanted to help her, too, but his brother's temper might do more harm than good.

Before Pierson could put his foot in it, Gray said calmly, "Quin, just calm down. We've all had a long day and I'm sure Eva's tired."

"Eva isn't tired," Eva said tightly. She continued to watch Quin intently from across the table. "You want to talk, Quin? Fine. We'll talk. But we are going to wait until everyone is done eating."

Despite the thick tension at the table, Pierson felt himself smile. *That's our girl.*

Quin had better be careful, Pierson thought. He was about to see the other side of Eva.

* * * *

The rest of dinner passed in silence. Eva didn't mind. She ate her food, knowing Quin would insist even if she said she wasn't hungry. When the table had been cleared, they paraded into the living room.

"Sit," Quin barked, pointing to the sofa.

He still seemed angry, but that was fine. So was Eva.

Once she was settled, Pierson sat next to her and handed her the wine. Gray sat on her other side while Quin pulled the sturdy timber coffee table closer to the sofa and sat on it in front of her.

"Talk to us, Eva," Quin demanded.

"I don't know what you want me to say." She looked from Quin to Pierson. "I've told you all about Tim." Her gaze moved from Pierson to Gray. "I've told you about my first boyfriend."

Finally she looked to Quin. "Now it's your turn."

"What?"

"You promised me that you wouldn't fly off the handle when you lost your temper. But every time you think I'm hiding something from you, you snap at me until you get what you want. So I think it's your turn, Quin. Why are you so overprotective? Why don't I know the first thing about your pasts, any of you?"

"That's not true, sugar." Grayson spoke softly, but Eva heard the thread of steel in his tone.

"I told you we were in the marines," Quin added.

"For ten years. What did you do in those ten years?"

Quin answered with a silent, stony look.

Pierson's fingers on her arm prompted her to look toward him. His usual smile was gone. He gave Quin a worried look before saying, "You're right that Quin shouldn't get so short with you, darlin'. But I don't think this is the time to go into it."

It was news to Eva that there was anything to go into. She'd just been following her instincts in confronting the Badons like this. It made her even more pissed off that she'd been right.

"I see," she snapped. Standing up, she glared at them. "So after I let you into my life—no, *make* you part of my life—you still don't trust me."

Both Pierson and Gray began to protest almost at the same moment, but it was Quin's voice that cut through and silenced them. "Sit down, Eva."

She looked at him for a long moment. His tone of voice brooked no argument.

Slowly, she sat.

Quin was silent for almost a minute, and then he said, "All three of us ended up overseas at one time or another, but we were in different units. They don't keep brothers together. We all worried about each other, but I'm the eldest. Pierson and Gray are my responsibility."

"We felt the same way," Pierson said. Eva became aware that he was still touching her arm. She grabbed his hand and held it. She reached out to Gray on her other side and took his hand as well.

"All of us lost friends," Quin said. "I thank God we didn't lose each other." He fixed her with a stare. "If I'm hard on you, Eva, it's not because I don't care about you. It's because I do. That's what family means to me.

"There was a man in my unit that I was often partnered with. Over time he became more and more introverted and I kept asking him if something was wrong. He denied it and I left it at that. He wasn't all right, but I didn't push him. I believed that if whatever was bothering him got too bad he would eventually open up and talk to me. He didn't. I should have pushed him more to talk. He committed suicide, and I will have to live with that fact for the rest of my life."

"Oh my God. I'm so sorry." Eva placed her hand on his arm. "It's not your fault, Quin. You tried to help your friend."

"I didn't do enough, Eva. I knew there was something wrong, but I didn't force the issue. Maybe if I had, he would still be alive."

"You tried to help him, Quin. You can't let the guilt eat you up inside. It could destroy you. You don't know what was going through his mind. You may have prevented him from killing himself then, but who's to say he wouldn't have just waited until you were home again?"

"I should have gotten him some help, baby."

"You can't help anyone unless they want to be helped, Quin. He would have reached out to you if he had wanted to."

"Thank you." Quin looked into her eyes, and she could see that she had indeed helped him deal with his guilt.

She could see his mind working and the tension in his body slowly eased. Maybe he was finally accepting that his friend's death wasn't his fault. She hoped so. Perhaps now Quin would let go of some of that control. He always kept himself on such a tight rein. Eva slipped her hands from Pierson's and Gray's. She edged forward until she slipped off the couch and knelt at Quin's feet. She put her hands on his knees and gazed up at him.

"I didn't ever tell you how I lost my father," she said.

He shook his head.

"He died serving his country. I was very young, but my mother taught me to always honor his memory." She interlaced her fingers with Quin's, relieved that he let her. "I understand why you would fight for the people you love, and I understand why you want to keep me safe."

Quin's face relaxed slightly. "Thank you, baby."

She sighed and stood up to scoot back onto the couch. Instead, Quin caught her hands and pulled her into his lap. "Much better," he said.

Eva loved the feeling of being held by him, but as she looked into his face, she felt all her doubts return. She'd had her moment of courage, and because of it she felt closer to her three men than she had before. But even that worried her.

She looked down at her hands. "Of course, this is what I'm scared of."

"Scared?" Gray repeated. "Of what?"

"This." Eva gestured to him and his brothers with a slight sweep of her hand. "Of caring too much and then having it all fall apart."

"It doesn't have to fall apart," Pierson said. "Do you think we don't have feelings for you? Do you think we're only in this for sexual gratification?"

"It's time you realized that we aren't just in this for sex." Quin's voice had gone back to being a dangerous growl. "Why can't you get around the fact that we are attracted to you?"

"It's like I've explained. Besides my first boyfriend and Tim's obsession, no one else has ever given me the time of day."

"So you still think we pity you," Gray said, "even after the picnic today."

Eva hesitated and then nodded.

Quin stood, taking Eva with him. She squeaked in alarm and grabbed his huge shoulders then looked up at his face. His mouth was tense, but his eyes burned as they met hers.

"That changes now."

Chapter Eleven

What changes now? Before Eva could process Quin's words, he shifted her effortlessly in his arms. Her world turned upside down. She let out a shriek and clung to the shirt which covered Quin's broad, muscular back.

"What are you doing? Put me down."

A slap landed on her ass, heating her denim-covered skin and flaming the embers of her arousal. Her pussy clenched, and a gush of cream leaked out to dampen her panties.

"Stop wriggling," Pierson growled and smacked her butt again as he hurried down the hall. A door banged against the wall as he shoved it open and then her world twirled once more.

Eva landed on the mattress with a bounce, releasing a soft "oomph" as her back connected with the quilt. She looked up to see three pairs of male eyes gazing at her hungrily. She pushed up to her elbows and, using her feet, scrambled back up the bed until her shoulders connected with the headboard.

Quin pulled his T-shirt over his head and threw it aside, and then he moved toward her in a way that she could only describe as a predator stalking its prey. A frisson of nervous excitement skated up her spine, leaving goose bumps covering her skin in its wake. He grasped her ankles and pulled her bent legs down straight. Then he pushed a leg between hers and nudged her thighs open as he caged her in with his body. Quin bracketed her by leaning on his hands and staring down into her eyes.

"We are all going to make love to you, Eva. If you don't want that, then you had better fess up now."

Eva wanted to demand their touch, but she didn't think her voice would work any more than a squeak. She was so turned on by their acts of aggression that she wanted them to dominate her even more than she wanted their touch.

She shook her head, trying to let Quin know she wasn't going to back out, but he must have taken it as a reply to his statement. He slowly pushed up from his arms and knelt over her. His look of regret and utter rejection caused pain to shoot through her chest. Just as he was about to move away from her, Eva grabbed his belt and the waistband of his jeans.

"Wait." She finally managed to find her voice, although it came out breathless. "I wasn't saying I didn't want you. I was trying to tell you I don't want you to stop."

"Be very sure this is what you want, baby, because after we all make love with you, that's it for us. Do you understand?"

Eva thought she knew what he was trying to tell her, but she wanted to be very sure before she answered. She raised an eyebrow. "What do you mean, 'that's it'?"

"What Quin is trying to say, sugar," Gray started to explain, "is that you will belong to us. Not just for a little while but permanently."

Her heart fluttered. "I understand," she managed to say.

Gray got onto the bed beside her and Pierson drew her gaze as he, too, climbed up on her other side. Both men were in their boxers, and she wondered when they had had time to remove their clothes without her noticing.

Pierson caressed her cheek with a finger. "What we expect from you, Eva, is for you to be open and honest with us."

"That means"—Quin tapped her thigh to get her attention once more—"if you have any worries, no matter how big or small, you come to one of us with them. No more keeping things bottled up inside and making yourself sick with worry. I don't care if you think you're imagining things or if you have proof about something, you come to us regardless. Understand?"

Eva nodded. Her heart was so full she didn't think she would be able to find her voice again. Tears pricked the backs of her eyes and even though she tried to blink them away she couldn't. It felt like her heart was brimming over with love and joy, and since she couldn't seem to talk and let these three men know how she felt, her emotions decided to find another way out. Moisture spilled over her lower eyelids and down her cheeks. Her vision blurred and she couldn't see their faces. Quin framed her face with his hands and wiped the moisture from her cheeks. Once done, he edged back off the bed and stood at the end. Pinning her with his gaze, he reached for the waistband of his jeans and pulled the fastening open then unzipped the fly. Not once did he remove his eyes from hers until he was standing before her gloriously naked.

Her breath hitched and stilled as Quin crawled up onto the bed again. He didn't stop until he was almost blanketing her with his body, but without touching her.

Pierson palmed her cheek and turned her head toward his. Before she could focus on his face, his mouth covered hers. He wasn't gentle with her this time. Pierson used his lips to separate hers and thrust his tongue inside. His flavor exploded on her taste buds, making her crave more of his masculine essence. Two mouths sucked on her nipples, causing her to moan into Pierson's mouth and writhe beneath the sensual onslaught. The hands skimming over her skin caused her to shiver and made goose bumps pucker all over her flesh.

When warm palms caressed her inner thighs, Eva couldn't help but give those hands and fingers easier access. She spread her legs wide as her pussy continuously leaked out copious amounts of cream. Sobbing with desire and frustration when Pierson withdrew his mouth from hers, she reached out desperately, needing to touch and anchor herself to someone as her arousal notched up another level.

One mouth released her nipple with a pop, and then the other did the same. She opened her eyes just in time to watch the three men trade places on the bed. Gray was now between her splayed legs,

Pierson was still on one side of her, and Quin was on the other. Quin pinched her nipple between thumb and finger, sending zings of pleasure shooting down to her pussy. Her vagina clenched, and another gush of cream leaked out. And then Gray lowered his head.

The first swipe of his tongue over her soaked folds was heavenly, but he avoided making contact with her clit. She thrust her hips up, hoping he would take the hint and lick her where she ached the most. Quin began to whisper in her ear.

"I'll bet now that Gray has tasted your cream, he craves more. Your pussy tastes so sweet, baby. One taste will never be enough. Do you like what Gray's tongue is doing to you?"

"Yes," Eva sobbed.

"Just wait until he sucks your little clit into his mouth. You are going to come hard and fast and Gray will want to drink down all your cum."

Eva whimpered as the tip of Gray's tongue flicked lightly over her clit. She wanted to beg him to make her come but couldn't find her voice. A velvety-soft touch to her cheek made her look in that direction. Pierson was up on his knees, his cock fisted in one hand as he stroked the tip over her skin.

"Open up, darlin'. I need to feel your mouth on my cock."

Eva pulled back slightly and studied the large organ, which had clear fluid glinting on the tip. Unable to stop herself, she flicked her tongue out and tasted his pre-cum. The sweet, salty taste just made her crave more. Inhaling deeply, she groaned as his musky scent assailed her nostrils, and she salivated for another taste. Relaxing her jaw, she opened her mouth and sucked the crown of his dick into it. Using the flat of her tongue, she licked the sensitive underside of his cock and hummed with pleasure when it jerked in her mouth and he groaned.

She wanted to be able to give Pierson pleasure, too, and began to bob her head up and down over his cock. On each backward stroke she hollowed her cheeks and lightly scraped her teeth over his hard shaft, suckling firmly on the tip. With every pass of her mouth over Pierson's cock she increased the speed of her bobbing and sucking. He grabbed a handful of her hair, and she gasped. She didn't know if he was using her as an anchor or just needed to touch her in some way, but he didn't force her to take more of his cock into her mouth than she could manage.

Eva squealed with pleasure when Gray began to attend to her clit with the tip of his tongue. While she had been getting into the rhythm of pleasing Pierson, he had held back and continued to tease her with only occasional touches to her sensitive nub. Now he centered all his attention on her aching pearl, and she was having trouble getting enough air into her lungs. Her chest heaved as she gasped, releasing a mewl of delight when Gray sucked her clit into his mouth. A sob escaped through her lips as he slipped a finger into her pussy.

He released her clit before speaking in a deep, gravelly voice. "You taste so sweet, Eva. You are so fucking wet and tight. I can't wait to feel you wrapped around my cock."

Gray added another finger to the one already inside her and began to pump them in and out of her cunt. Her cry was muffled by Pierson's cock when he thrust into her mouth again, and she squirmed as Quin's teeth grazed her nipple and he squeezed the other one. Eva was on sensation overload and could do nothing but give herself over to the three men pleasuring her.

Each of Gray's thrusts into her pussy hit that spot inside her that turned bliss to rapture. Eva whimpered and moaned, unable to keep herself from voicing her pleasure. The internal walls of her pussy felt tauter and tauter, gathering in on themselves as the rhapsody of the moment built higher and higher. And then she was on the edge of the cliff, not wanting the moment to end but unable to stop the joy as she cried out with climax. Her whole body shuddered and shook as ecstasy swept over her in huge blissful waves, and Gray didn't let up sliding his fingers in and out of her pussy or laving her clit until the last shiver ebbed.

"That was so fucking hot," Pierson gasped, pulling his cock free from her mouth. "I love watching you come, darlin'. You got me so close to coming with you, but I want to wait until I'm in your cunt before I fill you with my cum."

Eva couldn't believe how the dirty talk from her lovers made her satiated body sit up and take notice once more. Who would have thought her libido would begin to fire up again after she had just climaxed?

A large, warm hand gripped her hip, and she looked down her body to see Gray grasping his cock in his fist, aiming for her pussy. She whimpered with desire as the wide crown of his rod breached her delicate, sensitive flesh, stretching her wide. Arching her hips up, she tried to get more of his penis into her body. Eva felt almost desperate to feel him inside her.

"Don't move, Eva," Quin rasped. "Let Gray do all the work."

"But I need…"

"I know what you need, sugar," Gray gasped. "Just hold still and relax. I don't want to hurt you."

"You won't hurt me, Gray. I'm not made of glass." Eva thrust her hips up once more.

"Fuck." Gray hissed through clenched teeth and clasped both her hips firmly. "You feel so damn good. Don't move, Eva, or it'll be over before we even start."

Eva wanted to push Gray and make him lose control, but she also needed to come again so badly that she fought her urges and held still.

"Good girl," Quin panted and pinched a nipple between thumb and finger. "You are so damn sexy, Eva. What's it feel like having three grown men so horny they want to fuck you at the same time?"

Eva's imagination took over at Quin's words. What would it be like to have these three men inside her body all at once? One of them would have to penetrate her ass, another would make love to her mouth, and the third would fuck her pussy. Her vagina clenched with excitement at that image and released a gush of cream.

"Oh, you like the thought of that, do you?" Gray asked breathlessly.

"Yes," Eva moaned as Gray pushed all the way inside her, his balls resting against the cheeks of her ass. "I want you all to make love to me."

"Baby," Quin began, "we want that more than anything, but I don't think you're ready for that yet."

"Please?" Eva squirmed, causing Gray's cock to jerk inside her. "I need all of you."

"Oh shit," Gray growled and then rolled them both so that he ended up on his back with her lying over his body, her legs straddling his hips.

"Are you sure that's what you want, darlin'?" Pierson cupped her cheek, giving her a heated, hungry stare.

"Yes! Please. Now."

Quin moved off the bed and into the bathroom. He was back moments later and Eva saw him pass a tube over to Pierson. Popping open the top, Pierson moved behind her, between her and Gray's spread legs.

"Just relax for me, Eva. I'm going to prepare you to take my cock in your ass. Try not to tense up, darlin'."

A shiver wracked her frame when cold, wet fingers massaged over the skin of her anus. She clenched, making her opening tighter.

"Fuck, you're squeezing me like a fist, Eva," Gray groaned. "Take nice deep breaths, sugar, and when Pierson pushes, push back against him."

The more Pierson caressed her puckered skin, the more she liked it. Eva had never realized how sensitive the skin of her ass was until now. More pressure was applied to her anus, and a thick finger slid into her back entrance. Eva moaned and relished the small bite of pain the unfamiliar penetration caused. Pierson wiggled his finger, and she took a deep breath then pushed out using her muscles. His digit forged further into her bottom and then retreated back out until just the tip was resting inside.

"You have a pretty little ass, darlin'. I've been hankering to take a bite out of these sweet cheeks," Pierson panted.

A warm tongue caressed the flesh of first one butt cheek and then the other. She gave a squeak when he followed through on his words and nipped at each fleshy globe.

"Delicious," he rasped. "I'm adding another finger now, Eva. Try not to tense up."

Pierson took his time with her. Not once did he just thrust in hard or cause her any unnecessary pain. By the time he had her comfortable with the intrusion and stretched out enough to accept a cock in her ass, Eva was beside herself with desire. Her whole body felt like it was on fire. She wanted, no, needed to have all three of her men inside her. Without a doubt in her mind, Eva knew she would feel more connected to her men once they were all making love to her at the same time.

"More. Please? I need you all inside me."

"She's ready," Pierson growled.

Quin tilted her face slightly so he could see her eyes. "Baby, you may feel a slight burning and pinching pain, but it shouldn't be unbearable. If you have trouble accepting Pierson's cock in your ass, I want you to tell us. Okay?"

Eva nodded, her cheek brushing against the warm, firm skin of Gray's chest.

"Take a deep breath, darlin'." The head of Pierson's lubed cock brushed up and down over her rosette, coating her skin with the slippery gel. She inhaled and released the breath slowly. "That's it, Eva. Push me out."

Using her internal muscles, she did as commanded and then moaned when Pierson's cockhead forged its way into her anus. He held on to her pelvis firmly, not letting her move in any way. Once he penetrated through the tight muscles of her sphincter, he held still.

"Fuck! You're so hot and tight, darlin'. You feel so good," Pierson groaned.

When she began to relax and her internal walls loosened a little, he pushed in more. He repeated the process of holding still after gaining more depth until he was inside her balls-deep. His pelvis connected with her butt.

"I'm in." Pierson wrapped an arm around her waist and another across her chest, his forearm snuggled between her breasts. "Help me move her."

Between him and Gray, they managed to get her upright, with her impaled on two cocks, one in her pussy and the other in her ass. Movement to the side drew her attention, and she was just in time to watch Quin rise from a kneeling position to stand on the mattress. He placed his palm flat on the ceiling for balance, but because he was so tall, he had to bend his upper body over so his head wouldn't hit the ceiling. Grasping the base of his cock in hand, he shoved his hips forward and brushed the head of his cock over her lips.

"I need to feel your mouth on me, baby. Open up."

Eva didn't need to be told twice. She licked at the drop of clear fluid glistening in the eye of his penis and whimpered as his sweet, salty flavor coated her taste buds. Opening her mouth wide, she wrapped her lips around his cock and sucked, taking his shaft in as far as she could without gagging.

"Oh fuck yeah," Quin said breathlessly. "I love your mouth, baby."

Eva got into a rhythm of advance and retreat until she was bobbing up and down over Quin's cock. Every time she had just the tip of his dick in her mouth, she laved the sensitive underside with her tongue.

"Let us do all the work, sugar." Gray gripped her ribs just beneath her breasts. "You just concentrate on sucking Quin's cock."

Gray withdrew from her pussy until just the corona was resting inside. As he surged back in, Pierson retreated from her ass. The two men started off moving their cocks in and out of her body with a slow, easy pace, giving her time to adjust to being double penetrated. The rhythm ensured that she had at least one of their rods inside her at all times. But it still wasn't enough. She needed more.

Releasing Quin's cock from her mouth with a resounding *pop*, she pleaded with them. "Please!"

Quin sank his fingers into her hair and thrust forward slightly as she took him back into her mouth. "Oh, we'll please you, baby. Ramp it up, guys. Let's send our woman to heaven."

Eva mewled with delight as Gray and Pierson began to move faster. Their cocks shuttled in and out of her pussy and ass, and they increased their speed incrementally until their flesh made slapping sounds as it connected with hers. She began to bob faster over Quin's hard shaft and as she withdrew pulled her cheeks in to make her mouth tighter. His cock jerked in her mouth and he gasped.

"I'm gonna come, baby. Pull off now if you don't want a mouthful."

Eva reached out and cupped his scrotum with her hand. Quin growled and gripped her hair more firmly. She rolled his balls and lightly scraped the skin of his sensitive sac with her nails, causing his testicles to draw up close to his body.

"Fuck!" Quin roared. His penis expanded and then jerked in her mouth. Warm cum flooded across her tongue and shot down her throat. Eva swallowed rapidly, not wanting to lose one drop of his essence. When his climax was done, he stroked her face and his knees gave way and he flopped down onto the bed beside her, breathing heavily.

Warm tingles began to gather in her womb, making it feel heavy. Her internal walls fluttered and rippled, the tension in her body gathering in force as she raced toward ecstasy.

"Fuck yeah, sugar. Come with us, Eva," Gray groaned.

Each breath Eva took came back out as a sob as her body grew tauter and tauter. She was on the precipice but couldn't seem to fall over the edge. Then Pierson and Gray surged into her together, filling her body with hard cock.

Throwing her head back, she keened loudly as the pleasure spread from her womb to her clit and sheath and down her legs. Her toes curled. The keening grew until she screamed, her body jerking and shuddering as she tipped over the edge into nirvana. The cocks inside her felt huge as they surged in and out of her contracting body. Stars formed before her eyes and her vision turned blurry.

Caught up in the throes of such a powerful orgasm, she was only vaguely aware of Pierson and Gray yelling out as they both reached their release. Flopping down onto Gray, she closed her eyes once more, her body still giving the occasional jerk as the aftershocks of a huge climax waned. Her muscles totally lax with satiation, she felt herself drifting into sleep.

As she began to float, she wondered why she had waited so long to let her men make love to her. She had found more than heaven in their arms. Eva had found love and acceptance.

Chapter Twelve

Eva's stomach grumbled with hunger. Glancing at the clock on the office wall, she realized she had worked through her lunch hour. Saving the spreadsheet she had just finished entering data into, she closed the program, stood up, and stretched out her tired muscles.

Grabbing her purse from the other desk, she walked out into the workshop. All her men were busy fixing cars and were mostly out of sight. Eva didn't want to disturb them, so she just headed out and instead of getting into her car decided to walk to the diner to get them all some lunch since it was such a beautiful day.

As she walked, she thought back on the past two weeks. She felt as though she'd been living with her head in the clouds. The three Badon brothers spent time with her both alone and together, and they made love to her the same way. Every night she spent in the arms of her men, and she loved it. For the first time in what seemed like ages, she looked forward to every day.

She was only halfway to the diner when a car slowed down and kept pace with her.

"Eva!"

Looking to see who it was trying to hail her, she stopped and turned. The blood in her face drained away, leaving her feeling like she was about to pass out. Swaying on her feet, she blinked a few times, not sure she trusted her eyes.

"Eva," Tim called through the window of his car. He pulled over to the curb. He put his car in park. "What the hell are you doing in this small, out-of-the-way town?"

Eva was too anxious at seeing Tim to think coherently, so she kept her mouth shut, clutching her purse tightly to her chest.

"Why did you leave home, Evana?" Tim opened his door and got out. He didn't stop moving until he was within arm's length. "I've been too patient with you, Eva. It's time you learned where your place is."

Tim gripped her arm and pulled her toward his car. Finally coming out of her stupor, Eva struggled, trying to break his hold on her, but he was too big and strong. Tears pricked behind her eyes as pain seared into her arms where his fingers dug into her skin.

"Let. Me. Go. Tim," she growled through clenched teeth.

"No," he replied. "I have given you years to come to terms with our relationship. I'm done waiting for you, Eva. If you'd only stuck around we would be married by now."

Eva looked up and down the street. Of course, just when she needed help, no one was about. She was still too far away from the shops for anyone to hear her if she called out.

"Did you like all those presents I left for you, sweetheart? I know you know what I'm talking about." He dragged her to the car and shoved her through the open door and then followed her in.

Eva scooted over to the far side and tried to open the front passenger door handle, but it didn't budge. A sob of desperation escaped as she jerked against the handle again and again. The engine revved and the car took off. Reaching for the seat belt, she pulled it over her shoulder and pushed it into the slot until it clicked. She wouldn't be able to escape if his crazy driving killed her.

"Why are you doing this, Tim?" She turned to look at her longtime neighbor and, as far as she was concerned, her creepy nemesis.

"I told you a long time ago that you belonged to me. I've given you more than enough time to get used to the idea. I couldn't wait for you any longer. It was time I took matters into my own hands. We belong together, Eva."

The smile Tim gave her made her skin crawl with revulsion. Looking into his eyes, she found no warmth. It was like he had no soul and feelings for her at all. Taking a deep breath to try and calm her racing heart, she closed her eyes and thought about the men she loved more than her own life. No, she didn't belong with Tim. She loved Quin, Gray, and Pierson. Thinking of how much more she had to lose now, she felt herself sinking into despair.

"Why did you follow me here, Tim? Why are you taking me now, after I've been next door for years?"

"I think you know the answer to that," Tim responded with a serious frown. "You knew we would end up together, and then you left me. You weren't supposed to do that, Eva. You're too fragile to be on your own out here. You need me to take care of you and guide your life. You aren't supposed to be independent, and when I realized you were leaving, I…I lost it, Eva.

"I was bringing you another present when I saw you were packing and knew I had to follow you. You are more important than my business, than my anything, and you aren't supposed to be able to do this. You're supposed to need me for everything." His eyes had a wild, insistent look.

Eva gaped at him. Was this where his obsession came from? Some crazy fantasy that just because she had a disability she would be completely dependent on him and he could control her? She thought quickly, trying to come up with a way to bring him back to reality.

"What is your mother going to think when she finds out you've kidnapped me, Tim? You know she and my mom are best friends. Think about how your actions are going to affect their relationship. Your mom is going to feel so ashamed of you."

"Shut the fuck up." Tim glared at her as he yelled. Spittle flew from his mouth in his fury. "Our parents have nothing to do with what is between us. My mom has always loved you like a daughter. She will be proud of me when I finally make it official."

"You're delusional," she replied and cursed when she heard the scared quaver in her own voice. "I don't love you, Tim. I never have. You leaving me those things in my bedroom while I slept only made me more determined to avoid you. I don't love you. I don't even like you. You're creepy."

Shit, way to go, Eva. Nothing like goading your insane abductor!

"There is no need to play hard to get, Eva. You and I both know we were meant to be."

"No. I'm already in love, and no matter what you do or say, you can't make me love you, Tim." She spoke calmly but inside she was a nervous wreck.

"It's one of those men you work for, isn't it? I have been watching you and waiting for the right time to take you, but you are always with those fucking assholes. I wasn't about to blow my cover. My patience has paid off. Now I have you all to myself. Which one do you think you love? Quin? Gray? Or maybe it's Pierson?"

Eva must have blanched when Tim mentioned her men, because he gave her a knowing look and then smirked at her, but underneath that sneer she could see his rage. "Oh, no. Wait. You're doing all three of them, aren't you, you little slut?" The fury which crossed his face made her cringe away with fear. He glared at her, and it wasn't until the car swerved that he turned away again.

Eva thanked God they were no longer traveling through Slick Rock. If they had and Tim had swerved, he could have run down or hurt innocent people. Leaving town, however, meant that there was no opportunity for her to signal for help. Eva steadied her nerves and resigned herself to pay attention to where they were going so that if she had an opportunity to escape she knew in which direction to flee.

For fifteen minutes, Tim headed east on Highway 141, and then he slowed the vehicle and turned the car south onto 13R Road, which eventually intersected with 16R Road, which he then turned onto. Since she'd never been on this road, she had no idea where he was taking her. The trees were dense and the incline steep, and one side of the narrow road was a cliff face and the other was a steep drop.

While he concentrated on driving the narrow twists and turns the blacktop took, Eva gradually shifted her purse to the far side of her body until it was hidden from Tim's view. Carefully rummaging around inside, she sighed with relief when her hand landed on her cell phone. Glad that she hadn't removed it from silent mode, which was how she kept her phone while working in the office, she flipped it open and felt around the keypad with the tips of her fingers and then pushed what she hoped was speed dial one, which was programmed to Quin's cell number.

"Where are we going, Tim?" she asked in a loud voice, praying it was loud enough for Quin to hear if he had answered his cell.

"Just to a little place I found in my travels. No one ever goes there. We can have as much alone time as we need."

"I don't want to be alone with you, Tim. I want you to turn this car around and head back northwest toward Slick Rock."

"I don't give a fuck what you want, Eva. You are not going to get what you want until you agree to marry me," Tim snarled.

"And if I do agree? What then? Will you turn the car around and take me back so we can see a preacher?"

"I'm not fucking stupid, you dumb bitch. I know that if I took you back there you would yell for help the first chance you got. There is no way I'm letting you go now that I have you. I'm going to show you what a real man feels like when he fucks you. By the time I've finished with you, you'll be begging to become my wife."

"No I won't. I don't even like you. Now turn the car around and head back up 16R," Eva yelled.

"Don't you fucking yell at me, you slut." Tim reached out and slapped the side of her face hard. Burning pain emanated from her cheek and jaw where his hand had connected with her face. She bit her lip hard to prevent herself from crying out. She wasn't about to give him the satisfaction of knowing he'd hurt her.

Being careful not to draw attention to herself, Eva slowly pulled her cell phone from her purse and shoved it into the waistband of her jeans and hugged her door. The farther she stayed from Tim's reach, the better.

Approximately ten minutes later he slowed the car once more and turned onto a rough track, which was no doubt more suited to four-wheel drives than his rental car. Turning to look out the back window when he finally pulled the car to a stop, Eva saw that the car was hidden from view of the road. Even if someone drove this way, they wouldn't see the car. Fear skittered up Eva's spine.

"Why did you turn onto this dirt track? There is nothing here. Why are we stopping here?"

"Just shut up and get out. And don't try anything or I'll strangle you with my bare hands."

Her door was still somehow jammed shut, so Eva had to wait for Tim to unlock it from the outside. As she stood, her legs were so weak from fear they felt wobbly. Tim was nearly as big as her men, so she knew that if he wanted to, he was quite capable of killing her with just his hands. She clutched at the top of the car door as he stood staring at her intently. All of a sudden he smiled at her again, reaching out a hand toward her. Releasing the car door, she took a tentative step back and then another.

"You can't get away from me, Evana. So don't even bother trying."

Eva knew she had to act now. Tim was only a few feet from her, and if he managed to grab hold of her hand, she knew she wouldn't be able to escape his hold. Spinning around, almost blind with fear, she took off at a sprint. Dodging through trees, leaping over large fallen branches, she ran for her life. She knew she wouldn't be able to escape him because of her leg, but she had to try. Even though her right limb functioned normally, it was a lot weaker than her left and tired easily. The sound of Tim laughing close by made her dig deep for all she had. Pumping her arms and legs furiously, she ran as fast as she could. It didn't matter where she ran, and it didn't matter that she had no idea which direction was which. All that mattered was she get away from her insane neighbor.

The terrain was rough and she was running downhill. As the ground sloped away, she realized she was running too fast and her leg was weakening. Eva gasped with pain as a small branch wedged in between the metal bar of her caliper and leg. She cried out as the bough snapped, digging into her skin through her jeans, and she went tumbling headlong to the ground.

An "oomph" left her as the wind was knocked out of her, and even though she wanted to stay where she was and get her wind back, she didn't have time. Just as she pushed up to her hands and knees, heedless of the pain in her bruised chest and her leg where the branch had stabbed her, a savage hand grasped her hair and pulled her to her feet.

Tim wrapped her hair around his wrist, making her cry out at the sharp pain in her scalp as he turned her to face him, but it was also enough to get her oxygen-depleted lungs to suck in much-needed air.

"Try that again and I'll tie you up," he roared right into her face, his fetid breath causing her stomach to churn.

Eva whimpered with fear as he dragged her along beside him, careless of the fact that she was in pain and was having trouble keeping up with him. She prayed to God that Quin had answered his phone and had heard her give the clues about where Tim had taken her.

* * * *

Quin finished up changing the brake pads on the car and slid out from beneath the vehicle. Glancing to the clock on the wall of the workshop, he was surprised to see it was well past lunchtime. Usually Eva came out and asked them what they wanted to eat and then would head off to the diner to get their food. Although when it came to work, she was sometimes worse than them and would be so lost in her tasks that she lost all track of time. Going to the bathroom out back, he cleaned up and then headed to the office.

Eva wasn't there and neither was her purse. Although he didn't like it when she took off without letting them know she was leaving, Quin wasn't all that concerned. She knew their likes and dislikes and would sometimes get their lunch without asking what they wanted. He smiled in anticipation as his stomach grumbled loudly and walked back out to the workshop.

Gray was just finishing up replacing the clutch on a small hatchback and Pierson was wiping oil from his hands since he had just serviced the truck he had been working on.

"I'm starving," Gray muttered.

"Me, too." Pierson threw the cloth toward the workbench. "Where's Eva?"

"I think she's gone to get food." Just as Quin finished speculating, his cell phone rang. Unhooking it from his belt, he smiled when he saw the display. Eva was probably calling for their lunch orders from the diner. "Hey, baby."

There was no answer. His smile turned to a frown when he couldn't hear anything. There was some background noise, but Eva didn't speak. Then her voice came through loud and clear.

"Where are we going, Tim?"

The blood in his veins turned to ice with fear.

An unfamiliar male voice came through the earpiece. *"Just to a little place I found in my travels. No one ever goes there. We can have as much alone time as we need."*

He grabbed hold of Gray's T-shirt to get his brother's attention and then covered the phone's mouthpiece. "Call 9-1-1. Tim has Eva."

"What?" Pierson asked even though Quin knew his brother had heard him, too. He was in shock and fearful for Eva's safety just as he was. When Eva began talking again, Quin slashed his hand through the air to quiet his brothers down so he could hear. He thanked God he had such a smart woman. She gave him the general direction to begin looking for her, and then she actually gave him the name of the road and then the fact that they had taken a dirt track.

Putting his cell phone on mute but keeping it glued to his ear, he looked toward Gray and relayed what little information he knew. Then he pulled his truck keys from his pocket and headed for his vehicle. Pierson and Gray ran after him.

"Give me your phone, Quin," Pierson demanded as he slid into the passenger seat. "You can't listen and drive at the same time."

Quin reluctantly handed his cell phone over and took off with a squeal of tires. He sped through the center of town, being careful of the people milling about, but unless someone stepped out in front of his truck, he wasn't slowing for anything. They needed to get to Eva. She was in danger, and that he couldn't handle.

"Damon and Luke are on their way. They want us to keep out of sight until they get there. That is if we can find Eva and Tim."

"Like that's going to happen. We know what the hell we're doing. We trained for this shit when we were in the military," Quin snapped.

"Yeah, we did. And I'm sure the two sheriffs realize we aren't going to wait around for them to arrive. Nothing is more important than getting Eva back safe and sound," Pierson stated.

"Fuck!" Pierson roared with fury. "Eva just screamed. Floor it, Quin."

Quin put his foot to the floor and prayed to God they would get to Eva in time.

Chapter Thirteen

Eva reached up and gripped Tim's wrists, trying to alleviate the pain of his grip on her hair. Since she couldn't tilt her head to look down, she stumbled over small limbs and rocks as Tim dragged her along beside him. Using her short nails, she dug them into the skin of his hand and hoped she gouged his skin.

He stopped abruptly and almost threw her away from him. She cried out with pain as her lower right leg connected with a rock and her hands scraped on twigs and gravel. Just as she was about to push up from her hands and knees, Tim straddled her body and sat on her back. Since he was so much bigger than her and weighed at least eighty pounds more, she had no hope when he pressed against her. Collapsing on her stomach on the ground, Eva groaned when her cheek connected with the harsh bark covering a large fallen tree branch.

Her fingers clawed in the dirt as she dug in, trying to find purchase to escape, but all she accomplished was the discomfort of dirt embedded beneath her nails. Tim sank his hand in her hair again and pulled her head back until pain shot from her neck and down her spine at the unnatural angle. She shivered and shook with fear, but there was no way he was going to make her beg for her life. The bastard wasn't getting another word out of her. Eva wasn't about to waste her breath on an insane person. She would just have to bide her time and pray to God that her men found her and rescued her, because Eva knew she wouldn't be able to escape Tim on her own. She was no match for his strength and muscle.

Lying still, she calmed her breathing and tried to conserve her energy. Just as her brain kicked in and she began to search for something, anything she could use as a weapon, Tim's cell phone rang.

Before he answered it, he lifted up, flipped her over onto her back, used his body to pin her to the ground, and placed his knees on her arms so she couldn't use her upper limbs. Then he placed a palm over her mouth and pushed down firmly. With his free hand he unhooked his cell and answered.

"Hi, Mom, what's up?"

When Eva heard Tim talking to his mother, she began to struggle in earnest. She planted her feet on the ground and tried to buck him up off of her. If she could manage to unseat him then maybe she would be able to call out and alert his mom that he had kidnapped her. But he was too heavy, and he sneered at her as he spoke. He pushed down onto her as hard as he could, and using his thighs he squeezed them against the side of her ribs.

Eva pulled air in through her nostrils and stilled. Her struggling had only depleted the oxygen in her lungs again, and since her mouth was covered she couldn't seem to gasp in enough to take a full breath.

"Yes, Mom, I'm having a great vacation. I'll see you in about a week." Tim closed his phone and gave her a feral smile. "You and I are going to have so much fun, Eva. I have a whole week to spend with you."

Tim leaned down until his face was close to hers. Eva began to struggle again, but it was futile. He was just too big and heavy for her to get him off of her. When he bent his head and licked her cheek, she shuddered in revulsion, which seemed to amuse him. He sat back up and threw his head back, laughing almost manically. The hand over her mouth shifted slightly. Eva opened her mouth and sank her teeth into his flesh as hard as she could. His roar of pain and fury was satisfying, and she sneered at him when he pulled his hand away from her mouth. Turning her head to the side, she spat out the blood which had pooled in her mouth and then turned to look back at him.

His eyes were ice cold, as if there were no feelings inside him. In that moment Tim looked soulless to her. Then he drew his hand back and slapped her hard across the cheek and jaw. Pain radiated across her face, but she didn't give the bastard the satisfaction of crying out. She glared at him with all the hate she felt for him as the despicable deeds he had done to her over the last year came to the forefront of her mind.

Anger consumed Eva, and she let it. She needed to tap into the strength her fury gave her. When she felt like she was at boiling point, Eva brought her legs up toward her body with as much power and speed as she could manage. Her knees slammed into his lower back, and since she had surprise on her side, she managed to push Tim up and over her body.

How she scrambled to her feet the next instant she had no idea, but she didn't stop to question her newfound speed. She didn't even bother to look over her shoulder and see where Tim was. She took off running.

* * * *

"Gray, keep your eyes peeled for any dirt tracks," Quin demanded in a hard voice. "Eva said they had turned off 16R Road. Maybe that fucker turned onto one of the fire trails."

"This road intersects and turns in various places, Quin," Gray said anxiously. "How the hell do you know we're on the right one?"

"Because our woman is smart." Quin gripped the steering wheel so hard his knuckles turned white. "She practically yelled at the fucker to turn around and head back northwest toward Slick Rock."

"Thank God," Pierson muttered from the passenger seat. "Stop!"

"What is it?" Quin slammed on the brakes, bringing the truck to a screaming, smoking halt as the tires locked up.

"Reverse."

Quin slammed the stick into reverse and backed up fast, all the time scanning the side of the road looking for what Pierson had seen. And then he found it. Tire tracks on the shoulder of the road and several small broken branches where something large had snapped them almost in half, heading into the trees. He pulled the truck over into the gravel and dirt and parked. There was no way he was driving in and letting that asshole know they were coming. He and his brothers were going in on foot. With the element of surprise on their side, they would have their woman back before Tim knew what hit him.

Quin met Gray and Pierson at the back of the truck and was grateful that during the time they served in the military they had learned to be prepared for all situations. In a hidden compartment in the wall of the truck bed, he kept a locked box. Pulling the rubber liner away, he unlocked the compartment and then lifted out the box, which contained three loaded guns. After checking their weapons, Quin took off into the dense trees, Gray and Pierson following.

* * * *

Eva darted around trees and rocks, her breath coming out from between her lips in panting sobs. She heard heavy footfalls behind her and knew time was running out. Tim would be upon her in moments. And then she stumbled over something. A squeak left her mouth as her foot landed wrong and her ankle gave way.

She tumbled forward and down the incline, her body going ass over tit. Reaching out, she tried to slow her momentum. Stones and bark dug into the palms of her hands, but she was unable to stop her fall. So she tucked her head and arms into her body and prayed that she would soon stop.

Just as she began to slow, she lifted her head, and pain slammed into the back of her skull viciously. Eva saw stars and whimpered but she breathed through the pain, trying to circumvent the blackness assailing her. She had to stay conscious if she wanted a chance to get away from Tim.

A twig snapped right next to her and she tried to lift her head and squint through her pain, but her head was too heavy. A merciless hand grabbed hold of her hair and yanked, causing her to scream in agony as she was lifted to her feet. With blurry vision she stared in horror at Tim. He had a gun in his hand and it was pointed at her head.

"Don't ever try anything like that again, you fucking bitch. If it wasn't for the fact I want you as my wife, I would shoot you here and now."

Eva sobbed and gripped Tim's wrist as he jerked her and began to pull her back up the hill. She could barely see and she felt sick to her stomach. Her whole body ached and was surely bruised after her headlong fall down the steep slope. Sticky fluid trickled down the back of her head and neck. No doubt she had cut her head on that rock when it had stopped her fall.

Just as they reached the top of the hill, Tim stopped. He pulled her in front of him and placed the barrel of the gun beneath her chin. She swayed on her feet at the abrupt movement, and her vision dimmed once more. Taking deep, steady breaths, she fought back the dark spots which had formed before her eyes.

"Let her go, Tim."

Oh God, she must have hit her head really hard, because now she was hearing Quin's voice in her head.

The cold metal barrel of the gun was pushed so hard into the underside of her jaw Eva knew she was going to have a bruise. Her legs were shaking, and she didn't know how much longer she could remain on her feet.

"She's mine," Tim roared.

Eva struggled to see through her hazy vision and felt her knees begin to give way when she saw the outline of a man standing in front of her. She couldn't quite make out his features as the sun was behind him, casting him in a silhouette.

"No, Evana isn't yours, Tim," Quin replied calmly.

Thank you, God. It was Quin who was standing yards away from her. If he was here, she had no doubt that Gray and Pierson were as well. "She is her own person and you can't make her love you. Let her go and we'll all talk."

"Do you think I'm fucking stupid?" The grip Tim had on her hair tightened, causing even more pain to radiate into her skull. "As soon as I release her, you will be on me. Back up or I'll put a bullet in her."

Eva watched Quin back up a few steps through fuzzy eyes. She wanted to reach out and touch him. She hadn't even told her men that she loved them and now she may not get the chance. There was no way she was going to die with regrets.

"I love you," she blurted.

"See? She wants to be with me as much as I want her." Tim spoke calmly this time.

Eva wanted to scream that she wasn't talking to him but to Quin. She opened her mouth, but her words were cut off before she could speak.

"Is that how you treat the woman you love?" Quin took a slow step forward. "Look at her, Tim. She can barely stand. Let her go so we can get her some medical attention."

Eva cried out when Tim pulled her head back by yanking on her hair. His eyes ran over her face and he frowned down at her.

"Why did you have to fight me, Evana? Why did you run?"

The gun left the underside of her jaw, and even though she couldn't see where it was now pointed, she was in too much pain to care. Her legs buckled, and the grip Tim had on her hair released. She moaned as her bruised and battered body once more connected with the ground.

A loud explosion sounded, making her ears ring, and then she knew no more.

* * * *

Gray and his brothers followed the tracks leading to Eva. His heart was racing inside his chest with fear for their woman, but he pushed his terror aside and used the skills he had learned while in the military. Quin signaled him and Pierson to split up. He was to skirt around to the east while Pierson came in from the west. He knew that Quin was going to walk into the line of sight of Tim once they found him to distract the bastard. Just as they came to a small clearing, the fucker came up over the ridge of an incline.

Fear and worry pierced his chest when he saw Eva in the bastard's clutches. She was bruised from head to foot, and welts stood out lividly on each pale cheek where the prick had slapped her. As he crept around behind Tim and Eva, keeping cover amongst the trees, Quin began talking to Tim.

He cursed silently when he saw blood on the back of Eva's shirt. He couldn't see where it was coming from, and although he wanted to rush in and pull her assailant away from her, he knew he had to bide his time. Tim was now using Eva as a shield against Quin, and even though he had a clear shot, he wasn't about to jeopardize his woman. If he shot Tim and the bastard jerked his trigger finger while he held his weapon beneath her chin, then Eva would die.

Gray caught sight of Pierson on the other side of the clearing but knew his brother wasn't in Tim's peripheral vision. Quin was trying to talk the fucker into letting Eva go, but Gray didn't think the bastard's obsession with their woman would let him release her.

He signaled to Pierson with his hand, letting him know what he wanted Pierson to do. Just before Pierson moved forward into Tim's sight, he moved the gun from beneath Eva's chin and began to aim toward Quin. Eva collapsed to the ground just in the nick of time. Three guns fired simultaneously. Tim didn't even manage to pull the trigger. Quin must have moved lightning fast, because Gray hadn't even seen his gun in hand.

Three shots to the head was more than any human could survive. Tim fell and didn't move. The reverberation of their shots rang through the woods, then all was silent.

Gray and his brothers rushed to Eva. Pierson pulled Tim's body out of the way and then they all checked her over for injuries. The worst one was the cut on the back of her head and the one on her lower right leg.

"Call for an ambulance," Quin demanded as he whipped his T-shirt off over his head. Gray did the same and then they ripped their shirts into strips. Carefully moving Eva onto her left side, he and Quin began to patch her up as best they could. He undid and removed her boots and caliper then slit the pants of her jeans so he could dress the wound on her calf. Using a thick wad of what had been his shirt, he covered the deep gash and then tied a strip around her limb to hold it in place. Quin did the same to her head injury.

Just as they'd finished, Damon Osborn and Luke Sun-Walker arrived on the scene.

"Shit. Is she all right?" Damon asked.

"I don't know. She has a laceration to the back of her head, another on her leg, and she is covered with bruises."

"An ambulance is on the way, but I told the dispatcher we would meet them. The sooner we get out of here, the sooner our woman can get the medical attention she needs," Gray said through clenched teeth.

Quin leaned in and carefully lifted Eva before Gray could. He made sure her head was supported and then followed his brother back toward the road and their truck. Pierson stayed behind to give the two sheriffs a statement.

Gray got into the driver's seat after helping Quin get Eva into the back with him. He took off and pushed the truck hard, heading back toward Slick Rock. Just as he turned onto Highway 141 he spotted the ambulance racing toward him from the opposite direction. Flashing his headlights to get the driver's attention, he slowed down and finally stopped, preparing to transfer Eva to the paramedics' care.

Once Eva and Quin were on their way to the clinic in town, Gray climbed back into the truck, racing after them. He needed to make sure their woman was going to be okay and knew he wouldn't relax until he heard it from the doctor's mouth.

Chapter Fourteen

Beeping noises penetrated Eva's consciousness, causing her to frown. She wrinkled her nose at the clinical smell of disinfectant. She moaned with pain as she moved, aches and pains on her body making themselves known as she shifted. Her head was pounding.

Opening her eyes slowly to mere slits, it took a few blinks until she could get her eyelids to cooperate and open fully. Looking around the unfamiliar room, she realized she was in a hospital or clinic of some kind. Just as she pushed up on her hands, trying to maneuver into a more upright position, the door to her small room opened.

"Eva, you're awake," Quin said as he rushed to her side. "How are you feeling, baby?"

"Okay," she answered, her voice sounding dry and raspy.

The door opened once more and Gray and Pierson entered her room.

Quin poured some water from the jug on the table next to her bed and then handed her the cup. She took it gratefully and sipped until her thirst was quenched and her dry throat lubricated once more. Quin removed the cup from her hand and placed it back on the table and then took her hand in his.

"You have no idea how glad I am to see you awake, baby. We were so worried about you."

Gray and Pierson moved in close on the other side of the bed. Gray took her other hand and Pierson placed his on her thigh.

Eva couldn't remember how she had come to be in a hospital and was just about to ask her men when the memories of being abducted by Tim returned with startling clarity.

"Where's Tim? Did you get him to the sheriff's office?" She gripped the hands holding hers, fear and adrenaline racing through her system and making the heart monitor she was attached to speed up.

"Shh, calm down, darlin'." Pierson stroked her thigh through the cotton blanket covering her. "You're safe. He can't hurt you anymore."

She looked to each of her men and slumped in relief. "What happened?"

Quin explained how all three of them had shot and killed her old neighbor, and even though she was sad he had lost his life, she didn't feel guilty. Tim had brought everything that had happened upon himself. Not once in all the time she had known him had she teased him or strung him along. She did, however, feel sorry for his mother.

"Shit, I have to call my mom. She's going to begin to worry if I don't contact her again soon. I was supposed to call her last week when her and Jack got back home."

"Take it easy, sugar." Gray pushed against her shoulder gently when she tried to sit up more. "We've already called your mom. She and Jack are on their way here even as we speak."

"How long have I been here?"

"Since yesterday, darlin'. The doc wanted to keep you in overnight for observation. He was a bit worried about your head injury."

"God, I want to shower. I feel like yesterday's garbage."

"Okay, but how about you clean up when we get home? That way we can help you and you will have clean clothes to put on," Quin suggested and then said a little sheepishly, "We forgot to bring you clean clothes to wear."

"I don't think I can wait that long. I feel so dirty. I need to wash away his touch." She cursed her weakness when tears leaked from her eyes.

Quin moved closer and gathered her in for a hug. "Shh, baby, we understand. The doctor said you could go home as soon as you woke up. Now that you are awake the nurse will come and unhook you and we can get out of here."

Just as Quin finished speaking, the door to her room opened once more. Quin released her and stepped back when the nurse approached her bed.

"You're looking much better today, Eva. Now just let me unhook you and then you can get dressed and leave. Your men have already signed the release papers for you."

Less than a minute later, the nurse had her unhooked and then gave her a friendly pat on the hand and left without a backward glance. Eva still felt a little wobbly when she stood up and was very thankful her men were there to help her. In fact she didn't have to do anything, because her three men dressed her in the borrowed hospital scrubs and then Pierson carried her out to their truck. A quick glance around told her she was still in Slick Rock, which meant it wouldn't take long for them to get home.

Pierson eased her into the backseat and then got in beside her. Gray and Quin got into the front. Quin adjusted the rearview mirror slightly until he could see her and then he started the ignition and headed toward home.

Pierson once more carried her from the truck and in through the house. He didn't stop until they were in the bathroom adjoining Quin's bedroom. Sitting down on the edge of the tub with her on his lap, he reached out and turned the faucets on. As the bath filled with water he began to remove her clothes.

Gray and Quin walked into the bathroom just as Pierson pulled her last piece of clothing from her body. Quin undressed very quickly and then stepped into the tub. Pierson handed her over to Quin and then he sat down with her across his thighs as Pierson and Gray stripped.

Eva was still feeling pretty lethargic after her ordeal and injuries but was determined to wash the last effects away. She reached up behind Quin for the sponge and bath gel, but they were gently extricated from her hands.

"Let us do that for you, sugar," Gray stated and poured some of the liquid soap onto the sponge. He moved up next to her, lifted her arm, and began to wash her body. Pierson grabbed another sponge and began to wash her, too.

Once she was clean, she picked up one of her lank tresses. "Am I allowed to wash my hair?"

"Yes, baby. You only have a small cut on the back of your head and it has a small waterproof patch covering it. Will you let me wash your hair, Eva?"

"Please," she sighed.

Once done, the three men helped her from the tub and dried her off. When she was wrapped in one of their large robes, Gray blow dried her hair and Quin and Pierson exited the bathroom.

"Do you want to lie down in bed, sugar? Or would you rather go out to the sofa?"

"Sofa," Eva replied and snuggled up to Gray when he lifted her up into his arms.

The sofa had already been set up for her. There was a pillow near the end as well as a spare quilt. Gray eased her down onto the couch and then pulled the quilt up over her. "Just rest, Eva. We'll bring you something to eat and drink."

As she watched Gray turn toward the kitchen, her heavy eyelids closed.

A loud knock startled her awake and she jerked up into a sitting position. Quin reached for her hand, drawing her attention. He was sitting on the sofa with the pillow on his lap where he must have cradled her head while she slept.

"It's okay, baby. It's the sheriffs come to get your statement." He caressed a finger down her cheek. "Pierson, Eva's awake. Bring her some food and drink."

Footsteps sounded in the hall, and Eva looked to the sound. Gray led Sheriffs Luke Sun-Walker and Damon Osborn into the living room.

"How are you feeling, sugar?" Gray asked as he walked toward her and kissed her gently on the head.

"Much better. My head doesn't hurt anymore."

"I'm glad to hear that, Eva. Are you up to giving a statement?"

"Yes. I just want to get it over and done with."

"Ma'am, I'm Sheriff Luke Sun-Walker and this is Sheriff Damon Osborn."

"I know who you are, but thanks."

"Do you mind if we call you Eva?" Damon asked.

"No, please do."

"Okay, Eva, tell us how you were abducted and what happened."

Eva began to recite her story. She must have tensed up or gripped Quin's hand, because he pulled her up onto his lap, cuddling her with one arm while rubbing her back in a soothing caress with his free hand.

When she had finished her story, the sheriffs thanked her and left. Quin asked gently, "Are you all right, baby?"

"Yeah, but I'm glad that's over."

Eva sighed and rested her cheek against Quin's chest. She felt so loved, protected, and content, she didn't want to move. Another knock sounded at the door, but she was too tired to care who else had come calling. She heard Pierson open the door and then footsteps followed. When Eva looked up she was shocked to see her mother. "Eva, thank God you're safe." Her mom rushed over and hugged her carefully. Tears pricked her eyes and she closed them as her mom's love enveloped her. Her mother finally let go and stood up straight.

Eva opened her eyes and sat up again. "Mom, when did you…"

"Honey, how are you feeling?" Eva's mom asked as she sat down on the sofa next to her, not seeming to care that she was in the arms of a man, and kissed her daughter's cheek. Jack followed her mom into the living room but sat in an armchair across the room.

"I'm fine, Mom."

"The Badon boys told us everything. Why didn't you call me and or Jack to let us know what Tim was doing?"

Eva sighed. She could see the hurt in her mom's eyes, and that was one look she never wanted to be responsible for.

"I'm sorry." Eva took her mother's hand in hers and squeezed. "I didn't want to cause problems between you and Tim's mom. You have been friends for years, and I couldn't stand the thought of causing a rift."

"Evana Woodridge, you should know better than that. Ruth has known for years that something wasn't right with her boy. She used to talk to me all the time about some of the strange things he did. If you had come to me with what was going on we might have been able to intervene and seek out psychiatric help for the boy."

"I don't think that would have helped, ma'am," Gray stated as he rose to his feet. "The sheriffs contacted the military and found out he was discharged because he was schizophrenic."

"Oh, poor Ruth. She's lived through hell trying to get that boy help. Hopefully, once she has grieved she can get on with her life."

The rest of the day was spent with her men, her mom, and Jack. Eva wanted to tell her mom about loving three men but was waiting until she could speak with her alone. Her men had been a little more restrained with showing her affection since her mom and Jack had arrived.

But it seemed Eva still couldn't hide anything from her mom. After saying good-bye to Jack and hugging her mom, her mother surprised her for the second time that day.

"I can see how much you love your men, Eva. Which one are you going to marry?"

"Mom," Eva whispered so no one overheard her. "They haven't even asked me yet."

"Oh, fiddle-faddle." Her mom used her favorite expression. "It's only a matter of time. I expect a call from you telling me the date of the wedding in a few days. Now, off to bed with you. You look exhausted."

"We'll drop by in the morning before we head home. I love you, Eva."

"I love you, too, Mom."

Eva watched her mother and Jack until they were gone. Gray and Pierson had each come close and wrapped an arm around her waist. Quin turned toward her, taking her hand, and guided her back inside.

"You are going to bed, baby. You need a good night's sleep."

Eva let her men guide her to Quin's room and help her undress. Once she was in bed, they each divested their clothes and climbed into bed with her. She was surrounded by their heat and comfort. Her heart was so full of love she couldn't contain the words any longer.

"I want to thank you all for saving my life. I love you all so much."

"I love you, too, baby. We would have gone into the fires of hell to make sure you were safe." Quin kissed her reverently on the lips, wrapped an arm around her shoulders, and pulled her close.

"I love you, Eva," Gray whispered in her ear.

A hand landed on her thigh and caressed up and down her leg soothingly. "I love you, Evana Woodridge," Pierson stated in a voice deep with emotion. "Now close your eyes and sleep, darlin'."

Eva smiled and let the love her three men felt for her wash over her. She was so glad she had decided to leave home and had ended up in Slick Rock. If she hadn't, she might never have met the loves of her life.

Epilogue

Eva moaned as hands and mouths caressed every inch of her naked body. Hands swept up the insides of her thighs, parting her legs. A hot, wet mouth suckled on the tip of a breast and a hand tweaked her other nipple, causing sparks of sensation to shoot down to her pussy. Her vagina clenched and juices leaked out of her cunt.

When a warm, moist tongue laved over her clit, she sobbed with pleasurable desire. Hands caressed her stomach, arms, and legs, and then lips brushed against hers. She opened up when the questing tongue slid across the seam of her lips, asking for entry. Reaching up, she wrapped her hand around Quin's neck and held his mouth to hers, relishing his taste as he swept his tongue into her depths. By the time he slowed the kiss down and eventually lifted his head, they were both breathless.

Opening her eyes, she looked from Quin to Gray, who was on her other side, and down her body to Pierson, who was between her splayed thighs. The sun was up outside the bedroom window, she noticed. She'd slept soundly through the night and well into the morning.

Pierson looked up at her without removing his mouth from her pussy and gave her a sexy wink. He then added two fingers to her pussy and pushed them into her vagina as far as they would go. Using the tip of his tongue he flicked it back and forth over her blood-engorged clit and began to pump his fingers in and out of her cunt. The friction of his thrusting finger sliding in and out of her wet depths caused warm, arousing sensations to consume her sex and spread up into her womb and down her legs.

Quin sucked, licked, and nibbled down her neck and pinched her nipple repeatedly between thumb and index finger. All the while Gray was suckling on her other turgid peak as he caressed a warm hand across her belly and up her torso.

The coil inside her began to gather tighter and tighter with each advance and retreat of Pierson's fingers. Eva mewled with carnal delight and arched her hips, pushing her pussy up into his mouth. Just as the blissful climb toward climax started, Pierson twisted his fingers inside her and rubbed against the top wall of her sex. He sucked her clit between his lips and lightly scraped his teeth across her pearl. Eva cried out with ecstasy when he caressed firmly over her G-spot and then suckled on her clit strongly.

Her whole body jerked, shuddered, and shivered as she shot up into the stratosphere of rapture and her pussy gushed out her release. Her three lovers didn't stop touching and caressing her until the final spasm waned and she flopped back onto the mattress in supine relaxation.

Pierson crawled up her body and kissed her on the lips. As he shifted to kneel on the bed, he drew her up into his arms and onto his lap.

"I need you, darlin'. Will you let us make love to you?"

"Yes," Eva sighed as she clung to his shoulders.

Pierson lifted her hips until she was hovering over his hard cock and then slowly lowered her down over him. Eva groaned as he penetrated her body, and when her ass met his thighs she used her legs to lift back up, his hard dick stroking against the internal walls of her pussy.

He took a firmer hold of her hips. "Stay still, Eva. Let Quin prepare your ass."

Eva relaxed against his chest and breathed deeply. Her pussy clenched around Pierson's cock when Quin began to massage her ass with cool, wet fingers, and then he pushed inside her as her muscles loosened.

"I can't wait to feel your ass gripping my cock, baby. You are so hot inside you're nearly burning my fingers," Quin panted.

Eva whimpered and moaned as Quin stretched her out and then the pressure inside grew.

"I have three fingers in you, Eva. Are you ready to take me?"

"Yes, please. Hurry."

Quin shifted closer and then his cock began to push inside. Her ass burned slightly as the wide head stretched her flesh, but it was a good burn. With slow, short thrusts he gently forged his way inside and then held still when he was in all the way. Eva moaned and wiggled her hips. The two cocks in her body felt so good, it was almost too much pleasure to bear. She was so full but she needed more. Turning her head she looked for Gray and grabbed the base of his cock with her hand. He was already in position, waiting for her loving.

Leaning slightly to the side, she sucked him in and began to bob her head up and down the length of his shaft. As she withdrew to the tip she swirled her tongue around the head and laved the underside of his corona.

Eva moaned when Quin and Pierson began to pump their hips, sliding their cocks in and out of her ass and pussy. The sound was muffled since she had Gray's dick in her mouth. When she moved faster over Gray, Quin and Pierson kept pace with her. Instead of counterthrusting into her holes, they moved in sync so that she was either full of their cocks or nearly empty.

Gray caressed the side of her neck with his fingers and she sucked on him harder. He jerked in her mouth and she knew he was about to climax. Reaching out, she cupped his balls and rolled them gently in her hand. He moaned, and she felt his dick twitch and begin to expand. "I'm gonna come, sugar. Pull off, Eva," Gray gasped.

Eva ignored him. She wanted to have his taste in her mouth. Using her fingernails, she scraped them lightly against his scrotum and then squeezed his balls. Gray roared and pushed his dick nearly to the back of her throat. His cum shot out the end of his penis, coating her tongue and spewing down her throat. Eva gulped his seed and moaned when he withdrew from her mouth.

Pierson held her hips and surged up into her pussy at the same time Quin stroked into her ass. Quin's hands kneaded her breasts and then he squeezed her nipples.

Eva whimpered as the tingles and warmth accumulating in her womb traveled to her aching pussy and throbbing clit. The internal walls of her vagina began to coil and her legs trembled.

"I'm close," Quin panted. "Push her over."

Pierson slid his hand down her belly and rubbed her clit. That was all it took. Eva screamed as pleasure consumed her. Her pussy contracted, clenching and releasing, gripping and freeing around the two cocks in her body. Pierson clasped her hips and pumped into her one more time. He groaned loudly and shot her full of his cum.

Quin surged into her twice more and then froze. He shouted as his dick jerked and jolted in her ass, and then his seed spewed out and filled her back entrance.

Her men cuddled her close and kissed her. Quin eased out of her, giving her a pat on the ass before heading to the bathroom. Pierson withdrew from her pussy and sat back on the bed. He helped her to lie down and caressed her belly.

Quin came back from the bathroom and gently cleaned her with a warm washcloth. When done, he threw the cloth to the floor and climbed back into bed.

She gasped air into her lungs and waited for her breath to even out before she tried to speak. Pushing up so that she was half reclining and half sitting, Eva looked to each of her men and let them see the love she felt for them. Just as she opened her mouth to speak, Quin clasped her hand, lifted it to his mouth, and kissed the back of it. Gray grasped her other hand and placed it on his chest over his rapidly beating heart. Pierson sat up between her thighs and placed one of his large hands on her belly.

"Eva," Quin said in a deep, raspy voice. "We have waited for you for a long time and would be honored if you would consent to be our wife."

Eva gulped around the lump of emotion which lodged in her throat and took a deep, steadying breath. She opened her mouth to reply but stopped when Quin placed a finger over her lips.

"We love you more than we could ever express with words, baby. We've talked about who you would marry on paper and, since I'm the oldest, decided it would be best if you married me. So, Evana Woodridge, will you marry me?"

Eva pulled her hands from Quin's and Gray's and scrambled up onto her knees. When she was closer to all of her men, she reached out and took one of their arms and wrapped them around her body. Quin's arm was around her shoulders. Gray's ended up around her ribs, and Pierson's arm hooked around her hips.

"I can't imagine my life without you all in it. To do so causes an ache in my chest so fierce that I know I could never leave you. I love you all, too. I would be honored to marry you on paper, Quin. In my heart you are all already my husbands. I didn't realize how much I was missing until I met you all. You make me feel complete. I knew as soon as I met you that you were a danger to my heart. I'm so glad you didn't turn away when I let my insecurities get the better of me."

Eva kissed Quin first, then Gray, and finally Pierson. She would never have guessed that when she had run from her hometown of Sheridan she would end up where she had.

Eva looked at them and remembered the first day they had met. She smiled to herself. *Who would have thought a leg cramp would bring me to the loves of my life?*

THE END

WWW.BECCAVAN-EROTICROMANCE.COM

ABOUT THE AUTHOR

My name is Becca Van. I live in Australia with my wonderful hubby of many years, as well as my two children.

I read my first romance, which I found in the school library, at the age of thirteen and haven't stopped reading them since. It is so wonderful to know that love is still alive and strong when there seems to be so much conflict in the world.

I dreamed of writing my own book one day but, unfortunately, didn't follow my dream for many years. But once I started I knew writing was what I wanted to continue doing.

I love to escape from the world and curl up with a good romance, to see how the characters unfold and conflict is dealt with. I have read many books and love all facets of the romance genre, from historical to erotic romance. I am a sucker for a happy ending.

For all titles by Becca Van, please visit
www.bookstrand.com/becca-van

Siren Publishing, Inc.
www.SirenPublishing.com

CPSIA information can be obtained at www.ICGtesting.com
Printed in the USA
LVOW10s0105020415

432910LV00019B/515/P